**Susie Day** grew up in Penarth, Wales, with three older sisters, a lisp, and a really unfortunate first name.

Her many careers have included guiding tourists, professional nappy-changing, teaching small people how many beans make five and taller people how to interrogate the beans from a post-structuralist perspective, and being an eternal student. Along the way she's fitted in an awful lot of mucking about on the internet. Luckily she can now refer to this as "research".

She lives in Oxford, and is probably drinking a cup of tea right now (she usually has one around this time of day).

# Susie Day

# BiG WOO!

## Serafina67

## * urgently requires life *

**mlb**
MARION LLOYD BOOKS

First published in the UK by
Marion Lloyd Books,
An imprint of Scholastic Ltd
Euston House, 24 Eversholt Street
London, NQ1 1DB, UK
Registered office: Westfield Road, Southam, Warwickshire, CV47 0RA
SCHOLASTIC and associated logos are trademarks and/or registered trademarks of Scholastic Inc.

Text copyright © Susie Day, 2008
The right of Susie Day to be identified as the author of this work and has been asserted by her.

13 digit ISBN 978 1407 10686 1

A CIP catalogue record for this book is available from the British Library

Printed and bound by CPI Bookmarque, Croydon, CR0 4TD
Papers used by Scholastic Children's Books are made from wood grown in sustainable forests.

1 3 5 7 9 10 8 6 4 2

www.scholastic.co.uk/zone

To the Magnificent Niece Collective:
Rachel (with apologies for the lack of Maisie)
and Siân, who deserves a second mention and many more

| **Merry Christmas!!!**

Um. So. Hello?

I think you're supposed to be all "Tada! Welcome to ME!" in your first post. But I have met me and I am not really the "Tada!" type, so pff.

Anyway, lookie! I have a ULife blog now, woo, etc etc. I picked the name because you say the first bit kind of like Sarah, plus it is that witch in that film of that book. I always wanted to be Goth really. (Stop laughing now. Black is slimming, k?)

New blog exists because new laptop also exists, yay! Knew Dad would not stuff up this year, so poo to Mum and her blah blah don't expect too much. She has been a bit insane all day, actually. Who cares if the sprouts are all mushy, woman? Like either of us is going to eat them. But she really liked her scarf and the calendar-thing I made and got all sort of weepy cos I'd made it, which was all sweet. (Too much sherry, probs.)

So, I have stuffed my face and done thank-you phone calls and learned wi-fi (wi-fi is hard. Or I am stupid. What was so bad about wires anyway?) and now I'm going to sit on the sofa and eat lard and watch telly even though it's all old films and stuff. IT IS TRADITION.

Um. Feel like I should say "goodbye" now or something, even though probably no one will read this but me. And maybe Kym. Hello, Kym!

Wow. I am amazingly lame.

---

2.22 p.m. Friday 29 December | **grrrrrr**

Well, that sucked. Mr Shiny New Laptop lasted one whole day before going BOOM and there being smoke and explosions coming out of it. (Well, OK, not really, but you get the idea.) And it turns out that Dad got it through work (cos of VAT or something, which according to Mum makes him mean and evil) so we couldn't just take it back to PC World or whatever. So I was stuck with no laptop and him on the doorstep going "It's not my fault" and Mum going "It is so your fault GROWL ARGH" and me going "NOOOOOOOOO" in my bedroom with NO LAPTOP.

Christmas: season of shouting and explosions. Big Woo.

But Dad took it away and did some kind of magical mending thing and now the Shiny New Laptop is shiny again. Yay for techno!Dad. And so there shall be blogging.

Except I have done nothing except play on the internet and watch dvds and eat all the Maltesers out of the Celebrations box. Blah. I am going to be a bus by January. A bus with zits and bad teeth.

OK, I am SUCH a spoon. I was so thinking "OMG Kym hates on me woe woe cry" and posting mentalist replies on your front page and you thought I was some stalker. OOPS.

I am still kookygirl_x on MSN and AIM and all the others but on here I am serafina67. This is my proper grown-up blog for REAL friends, for documentarying my proper grown-up life, just as soon as I start having one. All the interesting/beautiful/non-zombie-librarian-type people are supposed to have a ULife now, they said so on Newsround. :P (Please to not be pointing out that I am not one of the interesting/beautiful people, k?)

This means New Blog Resolutions! (Yes it is a day early I know SHUSH.) Because serafina67 is the sort of person who Makes Plans and Is Decisive and Achieves Things, and I am her.

| | |
|---|---|
| Resolution #1: | Be brilliant and interesting and completely totally honest on here, daily |
| Resolution #2: | Make new friends due to the brilliant interestingness |
| Resolution #3: | No more "Incidents" |
| Resolution #4: | Make my sad mummy a happy mummy |
| Resolution #5: | Find way to not puke at mention of evil almost-StepMonster in time for wedding |
| Resolution #6: | Forgive Dad and, like, talk to him and stuff |
| Resolution #7: | Shrink self to less lardtastic size |
| Resolution #8: | Become boyfriended to prove unlardiness |
| Resolution #9: | BE HAPPY AGAIN BY APRIL 22nd |

Um. This is going to be the most outstandingly pathetic ULife of them all.

I am totally serious about that last one though. I downloaded a countdown thingy and everything so now I am stuck with it. I will do Resolutions #1–#8 and that will magically add up to make Resolution #9 happen, in a sort of breaking the rules of maths kind of way. And then I will transform into a tiny smiling head. Woo!

**HAPPINESS DEADLINE:** 113 days

Anyway, now you know I am just me and not a stalker, lollykyms. OR SO YOU THINK, MWAHAHAHAHA …

COMMENTS

**lolbabe**
UR so retarded! I was like WTF?
What is April 22nd? Thought yr birthday is in Feb?

**serafina67**
I know! I am the hopelessest. April 22nd = one year since The Incident. :(

**lolbabe**
lol, sry! R we allowed to talk about it now then?
Andandand U know Sasha and Naima and
Jaden and everyone read mine? so they can totally
work out who you are like I did? so U might maybe want
to Whisper this?

**serafina67**
Resolution #1: completely honest blahblahblah. And
anyway everyone knows I was a bit, um, mental last year.
Whisper = wha?

**lolbabe**

UR such a n00b! Whisper = so only your Top Friends
can read it? It is in like security settings or one of
those? But maybe that is not honest blahblahblah? lol

**serafina67**

noob?

**serafina67**

Ha ha, just looked it up on Wikipedia. I am like the
definition of newbieness. The newbiest newbie of
them all.

---

5.2 p.m. Sunday 31 December | **heeeeeeeeelp!**

OMG. Total. Clothing. Crisis.

My bedroom now has all the clothes I have ever owned on
the floor, which I have tried on about seventeen times in all
kinds of different combinations (pants on head and everything)
and NOTHING LOOKS NICE. Esp the pants on head.
Conclusion of this not-very-skientific experiment = the not-
looking-niceness is probably not down to the clothes but the
Thing that is inside them. :( And I have to leave in like an hour
because Mum has a pity-invitation to some Old People Playing
Monopoly Party at Francesca's parents' house, so she is taking
me and Kym there and we have to walk from there WITH
FRANCESCA to Sam Dawson's Actual Party, which is sort of
awkward and weird and ... gah. WHY DO YOU NOT
UNDERSTAND THAT I AM MAYBE NOT FRIENDS WITH THE

SAME PEOPLE AS WHEN I WAS LIKE TWELVE, MOTHER?

*cries*

I know I only started on the Resolutions thing yesterday, but can I be Shrunk and Boyfriended and have Happy-Without-Me-Having-To-Do-Stuff Mother now please? I promise to be good later?

Being on the internet whining about not having enough time to get ready is really helping, obvs. DUH.

I am blaming the Baby Jesus for this. If he hadn't been born I would not have eaten four mince pies for breakfast this morning. BAD BABY JESUS.

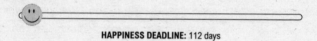

**HAPPINESS DEADLINE:** 112 days

---

10.55 a.m. Monday 1 January | **partaaaaaay**

OMG. Suckingest night of my entire life.

So Kym came over looking TOTALLY AMAZING and did my eyeliner for me so that I looked FAINTLY LESS CACK. And Mum was all "Don't you two look grown up" which obvs means "omg slutbags" in the language of Parent. I was waiting for her to go "Here are some frilly ballgowns for you to put on top just for when we go to Francesca's so no one will think I am an irresponsible single-mother-type-person" only we were running late, and apparently Being Late is worse than Bringing Your Slutbag Daughter And Friend Briefly To A Party. (Also she does not have any frilly ballgowns, unless she is a leading a sekrit double life involving frock-wearing, which is unlikely since what with me having no life at all we are spending lots of mother/daughter time on the sofa eating Doritos.)

So she drove us to Francesca's and made us get out so we could "say hello to everyone", even though the everyone was like all Francesca's grans and stuff, arg. Only when we got in there Francesca's dad was throwing this huge fit in the kitchen, because Francesca had told him that Sam Dawson is in Year 13 and there would be alcohol at the party. Well, duh. It is New Year's Eve, ppl?

So her dad was all "Did you know about this?" to my mum, who was all "Um ... no, not at all, gosh, I am shocked" etc, which is total bollards because she had just not even asked me about it which means she kind of knew. And he said Francesca couldn't go, so then Mum said I couldn't go, and then they said that Kym couldn't go, and Kym was like "Nuh-uh, you are so not MY parents" so they said they would ring her parents, so Kym was all "What am I, FIVE?" but she had told her parents she would be at my house all night so omg.

So we had to stay at their old people's party which was basically Cocktails With The Undead. Plus my mum. Francesca's mum and dad actually danced, in the middle of their living room. MY EYES, MY EYES! And they made Francesca play the violin like it was a sort of concert, with her sister playing the piano at the same time and everyone just standing there STARING, and she went all red, and Kym kept making me giggle and I had to run and hide in the loo and Francesca probably thinks I was laughing at her when I really wasn't, because in Year 8 Mum made me do piano and so I totally know how completely woes-makingly grim it is to have to try to make music come out of some bits of wood when there are people watching and waiting for you to stuff up.

And then Francesca's dad gave us each a glass of

champagne at midnight. WTF?

It was not totally rubbishness. Francesca's sister let us go up to her room to hide, and she played us tunes and stole all the good pizza for us (which I ate all of OMG FAIL). And at midnight we had to go downstairs and even though Mum was just in the next room she texted me "you look beautiful happy new year love you Mum x" which was quite yay and I texted back, and then I texted Dad to say HNY and he texted back "HNY love Dad" which was also quite yayish I suppose. (OBSERVE MY FORGIVINGNESS! I AM GROWING AS A PERSON etc.) And then Kym got a load of texts from other people going HNY and I realized we were saying hello to a whole new year on a green sofa covered in flaky pastry from miniature quiches, being kissed by someone else's grans and listening to Banging Party Hits 1922.

If the rest of this year is going to be like this, I am going to bed and not coming out again ever.

Oh, and Mum totally drunk-drove us home. Yay for responsible adult role models.

**HAPPINESS DEADLINE:** 111 days.

COMMENTS

**<u>lolbabe</u>**

OMG U typed everything? I told everyone we went to my uncle's and got mashed lol!

Andandand what was Francesca wearing?

**<u>serafina67</u>**

I KNOW! I was expecting her to be in a frilly ballgown for reals cos when we were friends in Year 9 her mum used to buy her all this total mingwear. But she looked sort of nice and non-dorky and everything.

Soz about everything messing up. And for telling everyone about our retarded social lives.

**lolbabe**

LOL I was meaning she still minged?

**serafina67**

LOL oops!

**patchworkboy**

You didn't miss anything. Dawson's was busted up by the neighbours phoning the fuzz at 11 because the music was so loud.

**serafina67**

PAAAAAAAAAAAAAAAAAATCH! It is you right? OMG you got raided. That is hardcore. Who was there? You were there! How come you were there? I thought you would think Sam Dawson was a townie.

**patchworkboy**

Sam Dawson is a townie. A townie with a house party and some free booze. And a load of policemen, as it turned out.

You type like a crackhead, by the way.

Picspam at my place. Clicky clicky!

---

1.46 p.m. Monday 1 January | **whine**

OK, am really bummed now. Not only did we not go to the

amazingest party ever (although thank god cos from patchworkboy's pics I think Sasha was wearing my skirt and her bum is a LOT smaller than mine), but now there is apparently the after-party clean-up party tonight. And where will I be? Stuck here with rellies. We have to go and pick them up and then go for a walk to NOWHERE AT ALL and then turn around and come back again, because apparently that is what families do on New Year's Day. I HAVE NO IDEA. But Mum is all pleady and says she will tie me to her ankles rather than deal with the grandparents on her own. Er, they are YOUR PARENTS, woman? That is quite strange. Although also fair, what with them being crumbly and boring. And ARGH RESOLUTIONS so I sort of have to be Magic Sera, Glowy Princess of Lovelyania, to hold Slumpy Mum-Queen's hand.

Maybe one day I will be in my own kitchen bribing Serafina Jr to stay when my mental rentals come to visit. Except my rentals would have to be TALKING for that to happen. (Plus, you know, birth. Urgh.)

She says, "There will be other parties, sera, durrrr," only the next thing will be the thing at J's next weekend and even if I was invited I will be at Dad's. When I will have to be Princess Sera all over again. Which will be quite confusing for him what with Evil Witch Sera of Betchistan usually being the one who comes to stay.

Grr. I am NOT going to spend the whole of this year in some kind of social black hole where all I ever do is hear about the cool stuff that happened at the bandstand while I was sitting here in my bedroom revising and looking at wallpaper with balloons on chosen by whatever colour-blind eight-year-old freakling lived in this grotpit before me. I am NOT actually a sadarse with no life. I am just made to look like one by my parentals.

Which is quite sadarsed, now I think about it.

Um.

11.22 a.m. Wednesday 3 January | **gah**

So I have already failed on the "daily" bit of my Resolutions so far. And the being brilliant and interesting thing. SURPRISE! But I have been ~~bored and lonely omg Kym where are you?~~ inspired with writing OTHER THINGS which sort of counts. I have decided to write a Very Thrilling Novel. That way at least I will have a fictional social life to pass the time.

It is about a girl called Anemone Kitson, who has auburn hair and emerald green eyes, and she is sort of a mermaid kind of person (only without having to wear a bra made of shells, ow), who fights crime/rescues drowning people/other things which I will explain when I have thought of them, with her best friend, Krystal, who is a detective (and has legs and everything). Word count: 206.

UPDATED: Actually her name is Juniper Gold and her eyes are blue. And she is not a mermaid, she is a girl made out of electricity who just makes herself look like a girl, and she can control anything electrical. Not, like, toasters. I mean like reading information off laptops and listening to people's mobile phones. And she is a spy and has Adventures with Krystal (who is a spy as well), and a boyfriend who has to eat loads of doughnuts so he is well insulated enough to give her hugs, but they can't snog or he will DIE. Word count: 323.

UPDATED: Maybe she isn't made of electricity, maybe she is just made of the internet. And she is a nurse. And all the doctors think she's really clever even though actually she just looks stuff up inside her head, and only Krystal knows the truth. It will be called *Zinnia Zmith: Googlenurse*. Word count: 0.

UPDATED: I think maybe I will write a short story instead of a VTN. :(

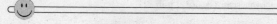

**HAPPINESS DEADLINE:** 109 days

COMMENTS

**lolbabe**

Ew @ fat donut boyfriend! UR so wierd and dorky, lol!

**serafina67**

This is what happens when you are not here! I go weird and dorky and REALLY BORED. Srsly, where are youuu?

**lolbabe**

Grounded still? Everyone are hanging out at Sasha's place though?

**serafina67**

I am sort of not talking to her. And I would feel ooky going on my own. Anyway now I am busy writing *The Flame-Winged Girl*. Word count: 401. Go me!

Sleeping, telly, avoiding marzipan, downloading things which crash the laptop and erase all my passwords, attempting to remember passwords, having passwords emailed to email account where I can't remember the password, hating self for being stupid, remembering passwords, hating self for being stupid a bit more. These are the things what I have been doing. Shut up with your laffing now, k?

Am now at Dad's (threw up in car, blarg) and am lying in a gigantic mountain of duvets and pillows at his flat WITH THE LAPTOP. LIKE I AM IN BED. Woo! Couldn't do this before. No more trying to use his desktop in his study with the weird mouse. And we did the pizza and dvd and popcorn thing and the Monster was not even invited. NER TO HER, HA!

Unless she was invited and just didn't want to come because I'm here. Urk.

Anyway SHUSH witch!sera because princess!sera is on Perfect Daughter duty and is doing Quite Well Thank You with Resolution #whichever one it was where I am nice to my dad. :P

He did his usual "We Must Talk Seriously about School and Feelings as decreed by Social Services and that woman on the telly", because it is like the law or something. Or it is since The Incident. And usually I would just shove more pizza in my face so he would get mostly cheese and mumbling about how Iamfinenowthankyoushush, but I was GOOD and did nodding and … um … Actually mostly we talked about movies etc because we were watching one. And then he was just such a BOY and went on about camera angles and "photography" and how there was some special CGI thing that some guy he used to work with does now, when of course the most important bit in the movie was Jake

13

Gyllenhaal's bum. (Luckily it was not a naked bum because I do not need to be sharing looking at Jake Gyllenhaal's naked bum with my dad. Just, no. But even his not-naked bum was definitely the best bit. OK, now I sound like a huge bum-obsessed perv. Um.)

Anyway that was still TALKING which = progress. Forgivingness/being nice to the Monster too can wait till next time, k?

I know it is a tiny bit witchy of me, but I wish he was staying in this flat. It is poky-small and I have to sleep on the sofabed with the big dink in the middle, which is a bit pants, obvs. And I know he only lived here in the first place because I was a supermassive brat, which is why he has these big black leather chairs sort of like the ones in *Friends* which say, "This is my Bachelor Dad Pad where you are very welcome to hang out whenever you like, for example two weekends in four as decreed by the custody thingy" and not a big flowery sofa which says, "My girlfriend chose this, don't come round ever as we may be snuggling". And really he was supposed to sell this place ages ago and move to where her job is, and he didn't because of, you know, all the stuff. But it is so pretty and hotel-like! You can flip the chairs up so you're sort of lying down which is dead comfy (though FYI makes popcorn fall down your boobs). And he's got new speakers to go with the widescreen TV and they make it seem like scary things are coming in through the windows, which is extra scary at his place cos it is in this supershiny sci-fi modern building with security buzzers and intercoms and special ops ninjas might turn up at any moment to blow up an invasion of giant spiders. ~~I have not been watching too much telly lately honest~~. Who would not want to stay here for ever, for reasons which are not at all to do with Monsters?

OMG, he just came in to say goodnight and I had to pretend I was doing homework. And he was all "Oh, I'm so relieved you're taking studying seriously, mocks coursework AS options blah", and I was all "Oh, I'm so relieved you didn't read any of that."

And now Mum just texted me to say "Remind your father I expect you home by 5, miss you, Mxx."

*eyerolls*

When I get home on Sundays she has always eaten all the biscuits. I have decided to believe that she goes up to Della in the flat upstairs and they have a miniature biscuit festival, otherwise that's just depressing. Even more depressing than there never being any biscuits left.

**HAPPINESS DEADLINE:** 106 days

---

1.28 p.m. Sunday 7 January | **i am pathetic**

OK, I totally know he's buying my affections and trying to piss off Mum, but OMG I HAVE THE NEW GODBOTHERER CD ON IMPORT AND A HUGE BIG POSTER. And he let me play it in the car. And he borrowed my laptop so he could burn a copy for himself. (Actually that bit is sort of weird and horrifying because, hello, so not at all supposed to be Dad music.)

AND (OK this was probably the more important bit, but I am shallow, k?) I asked him where the Monster was this weekend because she is still nowhere to be seen, and he looked a bit shifty and said, "I thought it would be good for us to spend some time together, just the two of us."

Obvs there was a big "and this would be because when she becomes official StepMonster this will never ever happen again" dangling off the end of the sentence which he did not quite get round to saying, which is a bit omgscary because three months from now = actually quite soon really. And they have "exchanged contracts" on the house (whatever that means) so he might be moving Far Far Away even earlier than that. But still. He did actually think about me, in a nice not-having-scary-agenda way. Woo!

Hrm. Have to get through wedding before I get to the Happiness Deadline. MUST TRY HARDER AT NICENESS. Will have to surgically insert smile on to face for occasion or something. Once it is over it is one less thing to go flaily over?

Have to go and eat whatever that weird-smelling thing is he's torturing in the kitchen. Blech. Apparently it is organic. This means grown in poo, yes? :(

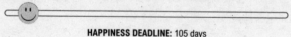

**HAPPINESS DEADLINE:** 105 days


COMMENTS

**patchworkboy**
Godbotherer?
OK, now I know why you type like a crackhead. You are a crackhead.
**serafina67**
OMG GODBOTHERER ARE LOVE!
**patchworkboy**
OMG PLEASE STOP KILLING ME WITH YOUR CAPSLOCK AND LACK OF PUNCTUATION

**serafina67**

LOL. Sorry. Sera is most dreadfully sorry to have misused ULife. Sir.

**patchworkboy**

Much better. I don't care if it's only Teh Intarwebs: those mysterious symbols on your keyboard are your friends. BTW, are you 67 for the reason I think?

**serafina67**

Mainly it is because there are a kajillion other people called serafina, woes. I thought I was being all clever when I thought of it too.

But yes, it is my old house number. Which was a stupid idea because now I feel mis every time I look at my own name. But I am stuck with it now. It is like when I called my hamster Hammy and then had to wait ages for it to die so I could have another one called something less humiliating. :(

I should probably not tell people that.

**patchworkboy**

You are not a beautiful and unique snowflake? *is shocked*

---

6.38 p.m. Sunday 7 January | **i am so screwed**

So apparently my really lovely time with Daddy and no Monster was so my Really Lovely Daddy could tell me his really lovely new plan for his Really Crappy Daughter. Except my Really Lovely Daddy is a LAMEASS and piked out of it totally and left it to Mum. Only apparently I have the SPECIAL LAMEASSERY so we can't even blame him for giving me genetic lame.

Everyone is VERY WORRIED about me. *sad face*

serafina67 is a Troubled Child and may need counselling.

serafina67 is, like, thrilled by this development.

Seriously, WTF? Like, it is not exactly news that I am, um, a bit rubbish? And a bit head-messy and likely to have a sad cry at unhelpful times and maybe not much liked by teachers lately? But apparently I am not just a bit rubbish. Now my school work is a Cause For Concern. Or I am a Cause For Concern, or something. And there is a letter from school which she has had all Christmas and AAARG.

Could we not just decide that I turned out to be a bit thick when school got a bit harder? COS IT IS NOT LIKE I AM NOT TRYING OMG. (Though did not put anything in Resolutions about school, revision, exams etc etc. Um. I will fix the school things when I am HAPPY again, k?)

Obvs no actual reference to The Incident, because there was nearly another Incident last time she mentioned The Incident and so we have a not-actually-arranged-by-talking-but-still-kind-of-arranged-somehow agreement to Not Go There. She has had enough Incidents of her own over the years what with supermarket weeping etc. But anyway me passing exams etc is much more important than anything else that goes on in my head, so that I will have PROSPECTS and a FUTURE and basically not turn out to be a single mother with a crap job and no life, i.e., her.

*flails*

Can hear crying in the kitchen now, guilt guilt guilt. I feel like I did that time when I was little and I knocked over that weird glass rhino thing in that posh shop and it smashed everywhere into billions and billions of little tiny sharp bits and broke a corner off a shelf, and everyone in the whole shop stared and stared and stared, and Mum went all red and had to apologize to the shop people, and they made her pay for it, and it was my fault except it was totally an accident and not anything I meant to happen and if I could have rewound time and just been a bit more careful when I turned around I so so would, but it was still my fault really and I felt SO awful.

Going to go and make her a cup of tea and make nodding noises.

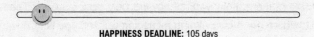

**HAPPINESS DEADLINE:** 105 days

COMMENTS

**lolbabe**
OMG have U seen sssasha's pix? I am on teh internet snogging the face off of J!
Soz about ur mum. Tell her U wont do it?

**serafina67**
My mum is not like your mum. Or maybe I am not like you. Anyway that will only make it a biggerer thing, is easier if I just go Yes OK whatevs.
OMG pix! Tongueasplosion!

**lolbabe**
OMG I know!

**patchworkboy**
The Glass Rhinos = Best Non-Existent Band Name Ever. I will download their single "Genetic Lame" immediately.

**serafina67**
Seriously, who buys a glass *rhino*? (It was like a million squids as well, OMG.)

**patchworkboy**
Glass zookeepers?
Your parentals and my parentals should get together. Then they

will all be in one place when we drop the bomb. :)

**serafina67**

Remember when we were little and they used to hang out together to drink gin and just locked us in your garden until the gin had run out? Supernanny would not have been impressed.

**patchworkboy**

It kept them quiet. Run along and play, now, parents! The children are busy building a fort and will see you later.

**serafina67**

LOL

---

8.01 p.m. Monday 8 January | **the ~~dog~~ rhino ate it?**

Where is my homework? Is it in the pile of things I did at the start of the holidays so it was all out of the way and I could put my feet up and relax and not have to worry about it? Or is it not there, because that pile does not exist?

I hate it when Mum is right. But I hate it more when she has to tell me about it, like, five thousand million billion times over. With "when I was your age" anecdotes. And sighing.

Today, however, involved large-scale coolness of hanging by the bandstand talking about all the stuff we'll do when we're not stuck in school being bored and getting told what to do all day. Kym is going to win X Factor, become mega-famous and then marry a gorgeous rich blond American (she doesn't mind who so long as he is all of those things) and live in a house inside the Hollywood "H". Bethan is going to make babies with Sol. Sasha's going to be a spokeswoman for blind children or something (lolz).

I don't know what I'm going to be.

So now I am talking to Sasha again and kind-of-talking to Naima, which is cool cos otherwise who am I going to talk to in Science? Is it Mr Davies? It is not.

No idea why I'm writing this down though cos you lot are the only ones who read this thing and you were there. WHERE ARE MY COOL AMAZING INTERNET FRIENDS FROM FAR ACROSS THE GLOOOBE?

Am just putting off finishing this essay thingy. Romeo, Romeo, bugger off and leave me alone Romeo.

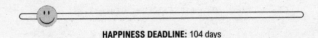

**HAPPINESS DEADLINE:** 104 days

COMMENTS

**patchworkboy**
I was not there. I was not even invited. For shame.
R&J: meet, shag, die, a.k.a. Shakespeare says Don't Do It,
Kids! This is all you need to know.

**serafina67**
OMG didn't think of inviting you! I suck. Though I don't think
you have to be invited really.
Haha, asked Mum about R&J and she says you are
depressing and unromantic. So ner. :P

**patchworkboy**
Bandstand + January = not my scene, ta.

**sssasha**
patch and sera, sitting in a tree, K-I-S-S-I-N-G ...

**serafina67**
LOL!

Yes Miss Kosminski, you can trust me to work on my project over in the library on my own. I am a good girl and won't at all be on the internet doing this instead.

Booooooooooooored. No one here to talk to but Francesca, who is obvs all La La I Am Studying I Cannot Even See You Invisiblesera.

Am going to look up gay porn and see if the network explodes.

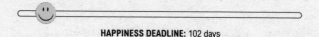

**HAPPINESS DEADLINE:** 102 days

COMMENTS

**patchworkboy**
Excellent use of school resources. *is in the chem lab doing same*

**serafina67**
You were in the chem lab looking up gay porn? (And OMG I so nearly got busted and was sitting there going uh-oh. I mean the blog part cos I was not really looking up porn.)

**patchworkboy**
Why not, you big old fag hag?

**serafina67**
I am not big! Well OK a bit since Christmas. (Fag hag?)

**patchworkboy**
*pats sera on head*

**sssasha**
OMG you two are so gay.

**lolbabe**

No, they are so doing it.

**patchworkboy**

*raises eyebrows*

**serafina67**

OMG!

---

4.45 p.m. Thursday 11 January | **overheard in a school toilet**

GIRL #1: That lipstick makes you look like a slag.

GIRL #2: Bitch.

GIRL #1: No, slag.

Heh.

That is the absolutely the most interesting thing that happened today. Except for when Mrs Talbot spent all of Business Studies calling me Georgina. Um, hello? I have been at this school for five years. And when I was in Year 7 you were my form teacher. Way to make me feel invisible, woman.

Yeah. Um. So much for this being my Deep and Meaningful Blog where I am all profound and stuff.

LIFE URGENTLY REQUIRED. IF SPARE ONE AVAILABLE, SEND AT ONCE.

**HAPPINESS DEADLINE:** 101 days

**lolbabe**

Georgina is that speccy girl in 11T with the stupid hair?

**serafina67**

OMG! SEND HAIRCUT WITH LIFE PLZ.

She is fat too. *cries*

---

6.33 p.m. Friday 12 January | **TGIF only not**

Pfff. Life sucketh. Have fun down the bandstand cos I will be here staring into space/BONDING with Mother. She has obvs been constructing Resolutions of her own because the kitchen is full of books called The Hidden Casualties of Divorce and Why is Your Child So Angry?

I am not angry, you twonk, I am just fifteen.

I am going to run out and buy ten copies of Why Is Your Mother a Mental? and leave them in obvious places around the house like the fridge. It is too late for her, though. She has lost it finally and utterly. She wants to spend tomorrow morning teaching me how to BAKE A CAKE. FFS, that is why Tesco exists, woman.

*is witch!sera today, apparently*

So yeah, if I am not in town tomorrow it is because I am becoming an old lady covered in flour and stuff. *headdesks*

**HAPPINESS DEADLINE:** 100 days

**patchworkboy**
*hugs you*
**serafina67**
*hugs you back*
**lolbabe**
OMG PROOFF!
**serafina67**
OMG KYM SHUSH.

---

9.12 a.m. Saturday 13 January | **busted!**

Ha – so it turns out my first meeting with the counsellor guy is this afternoon and he wants to meet me AND Mum AND Dad all together and so the cake-baking thing is totally her trying to make herself look like Best Parent.

STRANGE BOFFIN MAN IN SPECS:  So, Mrs Lady, how do you usually spend your free time with your daughter?

MUM:  Well every morning we rise bright and early and have tea and muffins on the lawn. Then I freshly iron our pretty frocks, and I carry her in my handbag all the way to school. At lunch time I arrive with a trolley and spoon-feed her little triangular sandwiches and home-made blueberry yoghurt, and in the evenings we like to knit and sing songs about vicars. We are like best friends and more like sisters than mother and daughter really you know.

STRANGE BOFFIN MAN IN SPECS: I see. And Mr Man?

DAD: Once a fortnight, we eat pizza.

STRANGE BOFFIN MAN IN SPECS: Aha!

That is the inside of my own mother's head. And they think I am the wonky one.

I know I should be all Yay Achieviness! about it but I really don't want to go to this thing. Especially not if they're both going to be there. They do not really do the sitting-in-the-same-room thing any more without it involving Giant Tension and both of them talking about the other one like they are not there, like that's supposed to be more polite or something.

I have no idea if the counselling bloke is going to be a strange boffin man in specs or not, but you have to be quite odd to want to listen to weird teenage-girl problems, no?

And I just read lolbabe's update and OMG! My ULife is all parental wangst and yours is all WHEEE DRUNKEN FUMBLING.

*wants more gossip NOW*

**HAPPINESS DEADLINE:** 99 days

COMMENTS

**lolbabe**
LOLZ! I am like grounded 4evah?

**serafina67**
Noes! *clings*

Well, that was officially the most head-breaky day ever.

It turns out my mum has spent half of her life being all miserable and in despair with WAILING and CRYING because she only has this one daughter and she wanted lots of kids but couldn't because she had miscarriages and Dad "had other priorities" (zomg) and now she is stuck with just me and it is TOO LATE FOR HER NOW.

Um, thanks? Glad I am like the fulfilling centre of your world. Although also OMG Sad Mummy again, and me not being able to fix that, and woes. Like, she has always been a bit of a glumface sometimes even from when I was small and we had a Supposedly Magic Perfect Family. But today she got really really gigantically upset, and it was about all this stuff I didn't even know about. Like, there could have been lots of babies before me or instead of me and I might never have been born at all, or had brothers and sisters, and all of it is like a bit of my family's history that got lost somehow. They had this whole other life before I existed, where there was Sandra and Bryan instead of Mum and Dad, and I don't even know those people. And they had plans and dreams and she was going to be a teacher, but she got pregnant and dropped out of her course, and then she lost it, and they wouldn't let her go back, so she never got any of the things she wanted, really.

And I am selfish and awful and even while I wanted to squishyhug her till she felt less mis, I still wanted to go "Waaaah, why me not good enuff?" So I didn't hug her at all, and Strange Boffin Man took notes on our Symbolic Lack Of Hugging.

AND Dad showed up late and then stayed for like TEN MINUTES or something because OMG not even kidding about them not being in the same room without it being WWIII. Although he did give me a hug which is probably also Symbolic but I don't know of what. But either way Mum got to look like superattentive!parent even with all the weeping because of her actually being, you know, IN THE ROOM, so all her cake-making was for nothing. Except for the fact that now we have cake, yay! (Also: it is kind of horrifying when you can see exactly how much butter and sugar is in Real Cake. But I am erasing that from my brain because coffee and walnut cake made by Mums and seras > coffee and walnut cake made by Mr Tesco, mmmmmm. And I made a big giant mess all over the kitchen and she didn't mind, and actually it was kind of lolarious and we are going to do it again next weekend when I get back from Dad's, only next time it will have CHOCOLATE in it. Woo.)

Anyway, the Strange Boffin Man turns out to be quite cute and unscary. He looks like Jamie Godbotherer (if Jamie Godbotherer was old and in a little beige room saying things like, "It's important to acknowledge the burden of all this negativity"). After a bit he kicked Mum out to go and de-mascara-trail herself in the loo, and asked me lots of questions about me, which was sort of appalling and nice at the same time, like when people at the hairdressers wash your hair for you and you can feel their fingertips on your scalp. I think he is probably quite good at his job of making people tell him their Deep Dark Secrets, anyway. Normally I am quite good at saying NOTHING AT ALL unless I want to, only with him I ended up quite blethery. I told him about the HAPPINESS DEADLINE (he says 99 days is not very long, wtf? Is aaaages), which meant I had to sort of tell him about The Incident, OMG. *quivers like small rabbit* And I thought he would be all "Hmm OK you are THIS Official Term for Crazyheadedness" but instead he was all "Hmm OK why is One Year Later so important quivery rabbit girl?" Which made me realize it is probably sort of because of Dad saying afterwards, "In a year's time, you will look back and feel completely different" and me sort of needing that to be true.

See how clever the Crazy Pete Man is at extracting knowledges from brains? Because even I did not know that. I even told him about wanting to write a Very Thrilling Novel, even though I have thrown away *The Flame-Winged Girl* (OMG stupid title) and have only just started on *HollowEyes* (Katarina Silver, silver eyes, can see into the future, 241 words) but he said I look like a "creative" person, and I said I was, kind of, and then he wanted to know what sort of creative, and OMG HE CAN READ MY MIND OR SOMETHING. And probably what he meant was "You are wearing odd socks and have icing on your top, hopefully this is because you are artistic/eccentric and not just filthy/disgusting, ew" but oh well.

BUT then he said that if I liked writing that would be good, because it would be useful to keep a record of how I am feeling and so I should start writing a journal. Ha! So now when Mum is all "Hello Laptopfiend, give me back my daughter" I can say I am under orders from the Crazy Pete Man and I am blogging for my mental health, yo.

Pff. Feel crappy and tired and all spun about. Think I have death cold coming on and want to crawl into bed and not think about Mums etc. But first, more cake. I am totally failing Resolution #7: Self-shrinkage, but have technically sort of tried a bit today with Resolution #4: Mum, and #6: Dad in a, um, totally failing kind of way.

*looks at deadline*

See? Aaaaages.

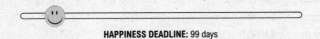

**HAPPINESS DEADLINE:** 99 days

COMMENTS

**patchworkboy**

Congratulations. You are now officially emo, little rabbit girl.

**serafina67**

Woo! I shall now wear stripes and mope a lot underneath my hair. ~~And eat carrots~~.

**patchworkboy**

The difference being?

**serafina67**

*slaps you*

**patchworkboy**

*is emo about being slapped*

**serafina67**

*is more emo about slapping you*

**patchworkboy**

*dies from emoness*

**serafina67**

*cries*

**patchworkboy**

*magically comes back to life using magic emo dust*

**serafina67**

*squees*

**patchworkboy**

*goes to band practice, sorry*

**serafina67**

*sulks*

**daisy13**

Sorry you had a bad day, serafina67.

I am dying. GENUINELY. Typing with one finger while lying on bed. All face is now made out of giant hurting nose a.k.a. endless tunnel of snot. Ewww.

In case anyone does not know patchworkboy is an angel and not a patchworkboy at all. He brings chocolate! He brings CD he has burned with all obscure weird stuff on that I have never heard of but is like cool! He actually sits in the kitchen talking to my mother while I am trying to crawl out of my hellpit and make myself look less like a sweating troll with a giant clown nose.

MUM:    My you have grown.

PATCH:  Um. Yes?

MUM:    So young man what do you like to do in school?

PATCH:  I like behaving well and being liked by teachers. Also maths.

MUM:    Jolly good. I will overlook your emo haircut and trust you will be a good influence on my trainwreck of a daughter. But not enough to let you go into her bedroom.

PATCH:  Fair enough. She looks like a sweating troll with a clown nose anyway.

She had him trapped for like twenty minutes and was ACTUALLY SMILING when I got there. Truly he is made of magicness.

WTF is the point of Vicks VapoRub? Now I am ill AND I smell funny.

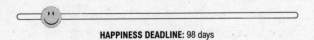

**HAPPINESS DEADLINE:** 98 days

31

## COMMENTS

**patchworkboy**

Not a clown, just a bit snuffly. Sorry I had to go: Joints gig on Friday and we need to suck less before then.

Hope you like the CD. Anything to drag you from the evil clutches of Godbotherer.

**serafina67**

Godbotherer are still love. But so is Zigg-ay.

Snuffly is not so bad. Sort of hedgehoggy-sounding.

**patchworkboy**

Rudolf the red-nosed hedgehog.

**serafina67**

NOOOOOOOOOOOOOO!

**patchworkboy**

*hugs you*

**serafina67**

You have my evil death cold germs now. Soz.

**lolbabe**

Did U get my txt?

**serafina67**

Yes! Only I am out of credit. *hugs internet which is all free and everything* So what is going on with you and J?

**lolbabe**

Sekrit! U like have to be in school tomorrow? Then I can tell you EVERYTHING?

So my giant nose problem is being slightly made a bit less evil by WOO! many many hours of daytime TV. I now know how to choose wallpaper that will not make my living room look like it is from like 1982, and how to make some weird-looking pasta thing with peas in it (seriously? ew), and how to make my whole family look like pikeys by YELLING at each other about My Love Rat Dad or whatever. I would never have learned these things in school.

TRISHA – 1: SCHOOL – 0

Mum came home for lunch so she could feed me soup. She is such a nutjob. I have a cold, I am not like a disabled or something.

Still no credit on my phone so can't text any of you back. But thx for asking about me! I am only slightly dying and will be back tomorrow unless I am too busy ~~watching Trisha~~ still being ill.

\*plays amazing mix CD from patchworkboy\*

UPDATED: OK now I am watching Midsomer Murders because when it started Mum said she used to fancy the detective man in it when he was in some other detective thing. To which I say OMG NEVER TELL ME ANYTHING LIKE THAT EVER AGAIN, EW.

UPDATED: OK now it is Murder She Wrote, which is about this horrible old woman with evil hair who has a typewriter and is nosy. I DO NOT UNDERSTAND.

**HAPPINESS DEADLINE:** 97 days

Trisha says we must all learn not to be judgemental about other people. Even if they have no teeth and do not have the sense to think "I am going on TV today, maybe I should wear clothes which are not three sizes too small/wash my hair/wash the rest of me" etc. Other people are so disgusting.

*is not at all still in sweaty PJs on sofa with greasy hair and smelling like Vicks*

Booooooooooooooooored.

Have nothing of actual newness to update with. Nose still huge. Ears now all hurty. Lungs making unusual creaking noises. Probably on brink of actual death any time now.

UPDATED: OMG the internets are so full of wrongness. Was poking through other people's blogs and now have found all the Harry Potter fanfic. Snape wants to shag Hermione? WTF?

UPDATED: Now Snape wants to shag Harry. Ummmmmmmmmm.

UPDATED: Werewolf Lupin/Doggy Sirius. MY EYES MY EYES!

**HAPPINESS DEADLINE: 96 days**

COMMENTS

**lolbabe**

OMG UR reading porn?

**serafina67**

I don't think it can count as porn when it is a werewolf and a dog. And I'm not reading it. I am sitting here pointing at the screen unable to move in FEAR.

**patchworkboy**

Yes, dear, we believe you.

**serafina67**

Oi! *slaps you* I am not really into werewolves.

**patchworkboy**

Glad to hear it. ;)

**daisy13**

Sorry to hear you're ill, serafina67.

**serafina67**

Um, thanks.

---

15.10 p.m. Thursday 18 January | **doctors are the suXXor**

Too cotton-woolly yesterday even to poke the internets for weirdness. Bleh.

I commented there but lolbabe, soz etc. J is an eejit anyway. And yes I know he can read this and I don't care.

Feel miserable and wretched and ick. Think this may have something to do with going to the doctor's and him poking stuff into my ear and listening to me wheeze by sticking his hand up my top, the big perv. And then he starts on the "how is your eating" thing. It is January you loon, my eating has been mainly chocolate and pies and such, which you can plainly see by looking at the balloon I have for a face. And you, Mr Doctor, cannot talk, what with your big saggy belly of grossness hanging over the top of your belt. I am on the "if you put food near me I will vomit on your shoes" ill-person-diet anyway, so ner. Resolution #7: Tiny skinnified sera WILL be achieved!

Without me having to do anything at all except be ill until April!

Erm. Maybe not.

Also: he started on some thing about "general mood" and it took me about four thousand years to figure out what he was on about, but duh, it is in my notes from last year. So he gave me this list of things where you have to answer YES or NO, and at the bottom it says, "if you answer YES to two or more of these, then you are suffering from depression", so of course I was all NONONOleavemealone, and he was all "Well you are obviously feeling much better yay."

What is the point of going to uni for a thousand years, Mr Doctor, if a photocopied sheet of paper can do your job? And, um, dude? I HAVE A COLD AND MAYBE A CHEST INFECTION. JUST GIVE ME THE ANTIBIOTICS, K?

I need to get old and grown up and far far away, like, now. Even if I turn into a mean old lady like the Murder She Wrote woman and wherever I go I will be surrounded by MURDERS and bad acting. Because that would still be better than this.

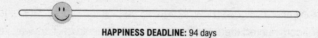

**HAPPINESS DEADLINE:** 94 days

COMMENTS

**lolbabe**

U should totally do him for sexual harassment? Like Simone Brasher did with Mr Cameron?

**serafina67**

*huggles you* Soz I am not there to be nice to you properly.

**lolbabe**

Is OK, didn't like him anyway.

**patchworkboy**

Get better. *sends flowers*

**serafina67**

*sneezes*

**dedkool**

lol lol lol u mental

---

4.45 p m Thursday 18 January | **spam spam spam meme meme meme**

patchworkboy tagged me to do a meme. And then had to explain to me what that meant. I AM TOO STOOPID TO LIVE, YO. *hides*

So, memeness:

*List five things about you that no one else knows. They can be as silly or as personal as you like, but be honest.*

Honesty, yay! See how I am achieving Resolution #1. Happiness shall be mine!

1) When I was little I grew my hair long cos I wanted to have bunches like Baby Spice.

2) I quite fancy that man on Blue Peter. I even asked for a Blue Peter annual for Christmas so I could have nice pictures of him and was really annoyed when I didn't get one.

3) Last week I dreamed that Francesca and Kym became best friends and hated me and when I woke up for a bit I thought it was true.

4) I used to have an imaginary pet squirrel. Called, um, "Squirrel".

5) Mr Phillips once touched my boob and it was totally not by accident.

ZOMG. I am a retard.

**HAPPINESS DEADLINE:** 94 days

COMMENTS

**lolbabe**

U R so dorky? Me and Francesca LOL :P

**serafina67**

I know!

**patchworkboy**

1) I reckon you would look painfully adorable in bunches.

2) No comment.

3) Is Francesca the one with the sister in Yr 13? She always seemed all right to me.

4) *Squirrel*? Mkay…

5) I feel neglected. I must be the only person in school who hasn't been felt up by Phillips.

**serafina67**

*pinches your manboob*

*blushes at the adorable thing*

---

6.46 p.m. Thursday 18 January | **hate hate hate**

Mother is a tool.

I am better. Is she pleased? Is she happy that she can stop

coming home every lunch time and ever-so-slightly mentioning how it is cutting into her work day but I come first because we-must-look-after-each-other-now-blah and she doesn't mind really no not at all but do try to get your craptastic lazy arse well again soon k? No she is not.

I have had four days off school so I should stay in bed all day tomorrow even though I am FINE. Which means I CANNOT GO TO JOINTS GIG.

Also: passive-aggressive much? She is like a PSHE textbook or something. *Sandy is saying one thing, but the way she says it means another. Use the cartoon strip below to suggest alternative phrases she could use to give her opinion directly, e.g., "Actually, I am watching that TV show, maybe you could tape yours?", instead of "No, no, it's fine, you turn over, I don't mind, *sniff sniff sulk*"*

Am going to throw stuff about now.

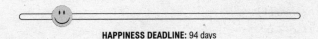

**HAPPINESS DEADLINE:** 94 days

COMMENTS

**patchworkboy**

Is OK. It's just a warm-up for next month. We will probably suck.

**serafina67**

NOOOO! You do not suck. I figured out about that extra track on the CD being you guys and you are the Best. Band. Evah.

**patchworkboy**

We did that ages ago, we're better now.

**serafina67**

Aaaaaaaaaaargh! Now I feel worse.

**patchworkboy**

We could always come and gig at your house. Personal performance at the end of your bed?

**serafina67**

OMG! *dies*

**patchworkboy**

Oh well, never mind.

**serafina67**

Whaaaaat? NOOO!

**patchworkboy**

Can't play to a corpse.

**serafina67**

*is alive*

**patchworkboy**

*tunes up*

**serafina67**

*squees*

**patchworkboy**

*sings* When you smile …

**serafina67**

*flails*

**dedkool**

YOU ARE ALL RETARDZ

**lolbabe**

OMG Jaden stop it.

**dedkool**

RETARDZ

RETARDZ

RETARDZ

**patchworkboy**

Look out, sera: intellectuals!

**dedkool**

U R DED

**patchworkboy**

So sorry, I meant INTELLECTUALZ.

**dedkool**

DED DED DED CU IN HELLZ

**serafina67**

OMG what is going on?

---

8.01 a.m. Friday 19 January | **love love love**

She changed her mind! WIN x eleventy!

Um. Now feel totally evil for yesterday. I am judgey and selfish and like some kind of stamp-footy spoilt brat!sera, and Mother is lovely motherperson who was worried cos apparently I did look really ill and now she is just happy because I'm not.

*hugs mother tightly*

MEMO TO SELF: Remember this feeling of niceness and do more things which produce it pls? Cos maybe Crazy Pete is right about Deadlines not being very far away. Urk.

And now I am pissing Mum off again making myself late for school because I wanted to come on here to sort of apologize. My stupid, it burns. :(

6.20 p.m. Sunday 21 January │ **liek whoa!**

OMG weekend of mentalness. Joints gig OMGOMGOMG. I should just type *flails* a zillion times, but it would not convey the level of *flailing* involved. EVERYONE was there. And Kym did my eyes all pandaish and AWESOME for me. *hugs her* And these girls from Year 10 were so drooling over patchworkboy while he did his God of Rawk thing and kind of flung himself about a bit, which if anyone else was doing in the lower gym would look dorky, obvs, but such is the power of Rawk Goddage. OH and he has New Hair! With like short bits and long bits and a green bit on the front. *fails at explaining*

And then Dad's, where I was all "Hooray I am Delightful Princess Sera observe me being effortful and Resolutiony in the direction of Fathers and their Future Wives." The Monster was actually non-evil and slapped Dad about for trying to "go for a nice walk" instead of going to the cinema which I have decided was entirely due to me and the effortfulness. She does still have totally horrifying taste in clothing and has to be coated in slap from head to toe like some kind of Unusually Old Shopgirl, but she is good at prodding him when he's being stupid. That is my job really, but I'm only there a little bit of the time, and otherwise he would probably just disappear into a hole made of pizza boxes and dad pants.

(Memo to self: Never ever contemplate dad pants again. Eek.)

She does do this thing where she wants to look you in the eye, though, which is sort of creepy. She actually grabbed my face and pushed my hair behind my ears and pulled my chin up so I had to look at her, and did that whole "There IS a girl under there!" thing, which is supposed to be kooky and sweet but is in fact a total violation of my personal space, yo. From there we are inches from "You know, I could do something with your hair" and her training me in the ways of clown slap and OMG, I am in that movie where the ugly duckling has a makeover and through the power of TAKING OFF HER GLASSES transforms into a ho. I think not, Monster.

This is the woman who is supposed to be taking me shopping for bridesmaidish things soon. *fears* She said, "I want something for you that is youthful, and in the fashion", presumably because of my well-known caringness about being "in the fashion" and all. It's not even going to be a big poofy cake thing, is it? It's going to be Lycra. And strapless. And OMG hideous.

BUT I DID NOT IGNORE HER OR BE EVEN A TINY BIT RUDE ABOUT HER BEHIND HER BACK except for on here but that is only so I am succeeding in Resolution #1: Honesty honesty honesty etc, so I am being good still really.

Also I achieved Talking with Dad (yay Resolution #6) and discovered that he thinks he is Mr Finger on the Pulse of Yoof.

DADDY-O:   So, what was the gig like?

ME:            "Gig"? You are an old man like Noel Edmonds and should not use this word.

DADDY-O:   I've been to a gig or two in my time. I know how to mosh.

ME:            WTF?

And then he found out the band are called the Joints and was all, "Yeah, cool name" about it, and then realized I am like his

DAUGHTER and was all, "Of course drugs are Teh Wrong" and was about to launch off into some awful story of his misspent youth when evidently he was some kind of smackhead or something, and then the Monster came back in and he totally shut up. I should ask Mum about this. Or maybe not. Still feel guilty for being a brat about the gig. Or the "concert" as she calls it, haha.

Am now kerknackerated from getting NO sleep at all on Friday and then not much on Saturday because I had waaay too much caffeine. Think I have had waaaay too much again cos I am bouncy like a mental. And now me and Mum are going to make cake and then I am going to write some of my VTN while eating the cake and then sit and watch telly with her ~~while eating more of the cake~~ performing sit-ups and, um, pretending that the cute one on Top Gear is our shared imaginary boyfriend. SUCK ON THAT, DEADLINE. :P Whee!

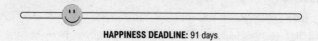

**HAPPINESS DEADLINE:** 91 days

COMMENTS

**lolbabe**

OMG have you seen Sasha's page? She has posted like this huge rant.

**serafina67**

WTF? Why does the world explode every time I am at Dad's? Is it true? Cos if so, er, illegal much?

**lolbabe**

I know it is like arrestible or whatever! But J says Faz says he saw pix on Mitchell's phone? So it might be true?

**serafina67**

OMG are you talking to J again?

**lolbabe**

Haha yes since Friday? Was U too busy drooling at Patch to notice? LOL

**patchworkboy**

Well, he is pretty cute.

**lolbabe**

OMG U R so gay.

**serafina67**

Everyone must stare at patchworkboy! It is like the law!

**patchworkboy**

That would explain a lot.

**patchworkboy**

I like your glasses.

**serafina67**

Freak.

**patchworkboy**

That's where you're meant to say "I like your new hair" back to me. Unless …

**serafina67**

NOOOOOOOOOOOOOOOOO!

*loves on it*

**daisy13**

That sounds like a pretty cool weekend. *jealousy*

**serafina67**

Thx. (Are you Francesca BTW?)

**daisy13**

No, I am daisy. Who is Francesca BTW?

**serafina67**

LOL. BTW = by the way. Noob!

---

5.32 p.m. Monday 22 January │ **erm**

> TEACHER: Blah blah oxbow lake blah. Now write essay and draw picture.
>
> ME: I was not here last week and have no clue what you are talking about.
>
> TEACHER: OMG serafina67 do I have to explain everything?
>
> ME: Yes. You are a teacher. That is your job.
>
> TEACHER: *explodes*

And then she went on for about half an hour about these parents who are up themselves and take kids out of school for a holiday and expect them to be able to just fit back in and YOU YOUNG LADY OF ALL PEOPLE cannot afford to waste time like that.

Er, cheers.

1) I was not on holiday, betch, I was ill.
2) I am not a YOUNG LADY. That is surely the name of some kind of horse or flower or something.
3) Could you maybe not slag off my mum to the whole class?
4) I was ILL.
5) It is an essay about a farking lake and you need to gain some perspective, woman.
6) Did I mention how I was ill?

*goes to watch Neighbours and sulk*

**HAPPINESS DEADLINE:** 90 days

COMMENTS

**lolbabe**

That was so out of order OMG! She was like yelling at you in the middle of the room!

**serafina67**

I know! I was like, hello, woman, do you have to unleash your flowing red tides of PMT on ickle me? Also, er, Sasha?

**lolbabe**

OMG totally! If she does not stop with the betching I am going to unfriend her?

**sssasha**

GET A LIFE was only playin @_@

**serafina67**

Well, don't, k?

**sssasha**

whatevah

**patchworkboy**

*puts up sign*

DO NOT FEED THE TROLLS

**11.51 p.m. Friday 26 January** | **we are cooler than you are, no we are cooler than you are, no we are, etc**

So I just had the best night in the whole world, and now I feel kind of meh. Erm. Emo points for me?

Kym was grounded AGAIN so I wasn't even going to go out, but then I was, erm, kind of persuaded to. :D And Mum was going out to eat curry (blech) with Della, so they dropped me in town and I met up with patchworkboy, and he held my hand and was all mumbly and I went OMG I APPEAR TO BE ON A DATE AND I DID NOT ACTUALLY KNOW THAT WAS WHAT WAS HAPPENING OMG.

But in like a good amazing brilliant way, obvs, except for me being just in jeans and looking quite cack and not having had any dinner. But we just went to the beach and hung out there, so everyone was in jeans, and it was quite dark apart from the campfire, which was very yay because HELLO JANUARY, and we got chips later. And I talked to loads of Year 12s I don't really know (OMGOMG but it was ok because patchworkboy knew them). And Momo from Year 13 had a guitar, and people sang stuff like Kumbiyah (sp?), which sounds sort of school assemblyish only it wasn't, because it was just a bunch of random people singing it because they felt like it. And there was hugging and stuff and wearing of Other People's Coats that were still warm and cosy inside from the Other People. It was like a little miniature music festival. (Not that I have ever been to a music festival, but that is what I am guessing it would be like, if it was tiny-small and on a freezing cold beach and made of win.)

And then when the fire died down I was all shivery, and patchworkboy was all shivery because I had his coat, so he sort of climbed inside it with me, and we stood under the pier and listened to the sea making swooshing noises ~~and, um, kissing~~. *happyflails*

Only then on the way home we cut through the park, and we went past the bandstand and I could see Jaden dancing around wearing no trousers and doing that thing he does which he thinks is SO hilarious, and Sasha and everyone were all laughing, and then the Year 12s I was with made some comments and were laughing as well though not in the same way, and then Jaden and everyone overheard them and there was yelling and pushing and nearly a supermassive fight and they were all looking at me with them and um.

I don't know. Um pretty much covers it. Can I be two of me plz?

But I can still smell the campfire on my hair, and it was sooo pretty with all the shadows all orangey on people's faces, and on the beach everyone was sort of unbothered about the whole thing, like no one was having to try really hard to say the right things or have the right shoes, and no one was all "OMG patch why are you with this dopey Year 11 girl", like no one was even fussed, except for me who was leaping in my head going woo! because I got to be a beach person for tonight and patch was still holding my hand and oh.

Why oh why do I not have a camera on my crappy phone so I can record these significant events for posterity? Must hit up Daddy-O for gifts, he is slacking off lately what with presumably spending all his money on his ginormous new palace/wedding cakes etc. Then I can fling endless picspam at this thing and it will be on teh internets forevah! Because one day people will stop reading Bloody Romeo and his Crap Dead Girlfriend and they will all sit in classrooms watching YouTubery from THE PAST that is now and reading BLOGGAGE instead and writing essays about magnificent us.

I had really better sort out a haircut or I will be in history looking like some kind of hairy mountain.

**HAPPINESS DEADLINE:** 86 days. Totally doable.

COMMENTS

**daisy13**

What is the bandstand? Your campfire sounds really cool.

**serafina67**

The bandstand is this place in the park where some people go to hang out. I don't know why we go there because you have to climb over the fence and everything to get in, and actually there is nothing there except an actual bandstand like for old people to play tubas on. So it could be anywhere really, just like a bench or something. But that is where one lot of people go, and another lot of people go down the beach, and the ones with cars go to the car park and drive about. I don't know who made the rules about who gets to go where, but everyone seems to know them anyway.

**serafina67**

Do I know you BTW? I just looked at your profile and it is like totally blank!

**daisy13**

I think I chatted with you on the Godbotherer forum and thought you sounded cool. Hope that's OK!!

**serafina67**

I HAVE INTERNET FRIENDS YAY!

*coughs and attempts to recover Air Of Coolness*

Though am kind of over GB now. Jamie is cute but the music sucks.

**daisy13**

Who do you like now then?

**serafina67**

THE JOINTS!!! (They are like the school band, you would not know them.)

**patchworkboy**

Sorry, didn't realize that "Please come to the beach with me?" was so hard to understand. ;-P I will be more specific next time.

Sorry about all the hoohah, too. Nobody was talking about you.

**serafina67**

I know. But it is still sort of um.

Next time? *squees*

You do know you are never ever getting this coat back, right? *snuggles in it*

---

6.37 p.m. Saturday 27 January | **tinsel nipples**

So I had my second lovely trip to the Teenage Mentalist's Brain Doctor today. Cute Boffin Man was wearing a very upsetting jumper with little curly knitting across the chest like someone had put tinsel across his nipples. I don't think he should do distracting things like that because every now and then he says, "What are you thinking about right now?" and I have to make up something about Oh My Angsty Teenage Torment so I don't have to say I AM THINKING ABOUT YOUR NIPPLES. Neither one of us is qualified to deal with that, Cute Boffin Man, and you know it.

He was all interested in my "diary" and I was like yep, I write in it every day (which I see now looking back through my old posts is entirely a lie – think I was just spamming other people's with comments instead, oops). And then he said the important thing was that it was something just for me, that no one else knew about, where I could be completely honest, because sometimes it's hard to do talking like this face to face, and I swear he knew about the nipple thing somehow. He really for true has some kind of scary mental X-ray vision. Ick. He was probably just filling up the time really, cos my brain went into whatwhowhatbzuh? mode and I had no idea what to say and ended up talking about the Monster and how I am Trying To Like Her. So he was all "What do you like about her then?" which was a bit tricky so I ended up saying how I like how she lets me choose whether we have Chinese or pizza or whatever (which is sort of likeable, y/y?) and he just kind of nodded and then went "Have you ever considered self-harming?" and I went kjsehrawehfjdsoa3q???

Er, no. Not until NOW, you loon.

And then he said he asked because I don't show off my arms, which makes me think he must be some kind of arm-related pervert who only gets off on like elbows and such. I swear there must be like a billion perfectly fine people out there who spend like twenty minutes in the presence of these shrinkydinks and come out weeping over their Mentalist Hell.

He asked me about the VTN too, which I forgot to say before is now about Genevieva Tristesse (raven hair, tragically pale) who is dying and bedridden (LOL you can so tell I started it when I was poorly). Only when she is asleep her body can go off without her sort of like astral projection, so she has to leave instructions with her manservant Drinkwater for what she needs to do when she is asleep, like "Take me to the castle and look in the wooden chest, where there are evil plots against the King!" type stuff. And Drinkwater has to remember to bring her back or she could wake up in like a pond or something. And she LOVES Drinkwater but there is the whole dying/bedridden thing in the way and so she never says, but obvs we know that he loves her too and it will end with loads of snoggage. Word count: 1,145. But Crazy Pete just sort of nodded and wrote things down and I couldn't tell at all what he would have written because he has the smoothest, vaguest face in the universe. Probably "Memo to self: Next time, do not ask the weird boring girl about her Very Tosswitted Novel". :(

Oh, and I am "articulating some food issues relating to self-esteem". Which I think is supposed to mean that I am a fat cow.

Yes, that helped my self-esteem. Danke schon, Herr Doktor!

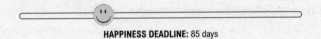

**HAPPINESS DEADLINE:** 85 days

## COMMENTS

**patchworkboy**
*hugs*

**sssasha**
OMG you are a proper mental

**serafina67**
Ummm thx.

**patchworkboy**
Not mental. Just emo.

**serafina67**
YAY! Like the kool kidzzzz. Are you coming over?

**lolbabe**

If  U R srs about the weight thing you should meet my two
best friends, ana and mia ˙;)

**serafina67**

? Are they in year 12? *cries at loss of Best Fwend status*

**lolbabe**

LOL duh! Err just google?

**serafina67**

OMG! Those pix are gross and deeply deeply wrong. I
know I am a bit lardy but, um, ribcages? Ew.

---

12.21 p.m. Sunday 28 January | **moral dilemma**

I feel really weird putting this on here because I know who will read
it, only I thought about it for ages and talked about it with
patchworkboy last night (um yeah soz about all that but you have
the Giant Brain and all), and I thought this was like a way to do it
where I could say what I wanted to say and not get into a row or a
fight or whatever, because I suck in those situations and will end up
just going, "Yes you are right I am wrong silly me" which will not
help.

So.

I have looked at all these pro-ana sites and they are really really
scary and upsetting. Cos all these girls are typing, "Go me I only
ate 400 cals today and I threw those up after anyway and then went
for a run." And then these others are commenting back with, "That's
OK but you will have absorbed some of those cals so you should

really go for another run or maybe row as that burns up more." And there are "thinspirational images" of people who look like they are in our history textbook from famines and death camps and stuff.

I know I am not exactly the most perfect-looking person in the world and I could probably walk around with a bag over my head for ever and be a lot happier, but, um, WTF? 400 cals is like some biscuits or something. I have a horrible body but those people look sick and awful and about to die. And the people who are commenting are only doing it to make themselves feel better about what they're doing and so they can show off and go, "Look at me, all I have eaten is half an apple and two ryvitas in a week" and make the other people feel bad.

And I feel really stupid because now there are loads of really obvious things that I should have noticed were like SIGNS. Like never coming round for dinner with Mum, and cancelling things, and all the "lalalagrounded" only not being. I just thought it was me who was being avoided. Because I am selfish and navel-gazey. But I can't be selfish and navel-gazey about this, because when I was all hopeless and drowning in life last year, no one said anything or did anything. And I totally get why, because zomg AWKWARD? and I didn't really want to talk about it, but it would have been nice to be asked, maybe. So maybe I understand a bit and could help or something?

So I just wanted to say that these sites look like really bad and ana is really bad (like in a "Oh no I am worried" way, not in a "You are bad" way, obvs) and I really wish that anyone reading this who has ana or mia gets some help. And if they want someone to talk to as a friend then I will totally be there for them.

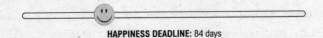

**HAPPINESS DEADLINE:** 84 days

## COMMENTS

**daisy13**

That's really kind of you to be so worried about your friend.
I'm sure you look much nicer than you think.

**serafina67**

That would be because you have never seen the
hideousness that is me. Here's my pic: <u>clicky!</u>

**daisy13**

Funny!! I bet you're beautiful really.

**serafina67**

Not very tall with brown hair that is too long and clear signs
of chocolate-consumption in the bottom region, resulting in
jiggliness. :(

**daisy13**

Lots of people like girls with curves. :)

Comment deleted by serafina67 7.42 p.m.

Comment deleted by serafina67 7.47 p.m.

Comment deleted by serafina67 7.59 p.m.

---

6.02 p.m. Sunday 28 January | **FU**

I'm not taking it down. I'm trying to do a good thing for someone
and I don't think trying to help someone who has an ILLNESS can
be a bad thing, k?

I am not the one with the problem here.

COMMENTS

**sssasha**

OMG srsly take it down

**serafina67**

It's my ULife, I can put up whatever I want. I didn't put any
names in it anyway.

**sssasha**

U dint have to whole school knows now.

**serafina67**

That's not my fault. Maybe it will help THAT PERSON to get
some help.

**sssasha**

UR the one who needs help fat hor

> Comment deleted by serafina67 6.38 p.m.
>
> Comment deleted by serafina67 7.01 p.m.
>
> Comment deleted by serafina67 7.06 p.m.
>
> Comment deleted by serafina67 7.28 p.m.
>
> Comment deleted by serafina67 7.40 p.m.

**patchworkboy**

Do I smell flames?

**serafina67**

*puts on fire helmet*

**daisy13**

It sounds like people are giving you a hard time. I hope
you're OK. If you need a friend to talk to, I'm a good
listener!!

**serafina67**

Thx. Nice to know not everyone thinks I'm a total betch.

**daisy13**

(hugs)

---

5.42 p.m. Monday 29 January | **to straighten things out**

OK, so apparently trying to be a good friend to someone = being an evil cowbag who deserves to be cornered on the way home and like THREATENED. Kthx? And how exactly is that helping her?

Anyway I can't make you STFU at school but I've found out how to post this so you can't comment, so there's no point you trying to spam me to death. And thank you to whoever posted the link all over everywhere and asked for trolls to spam me: that was really mature. I have deleted that email addy now so there's no point anyway.

All I was trying to do was help someone. I cannot be the only person to have looked at a pro-ana site and thought "Eww". And maybe I should've spoken to That Person rather than posting what I thought here, but I didn't know that and I thought this would be kinder and I was just trying to do the right thing. And I was talking generally anyway as well as trying to HELP that person.

I wish I could say this better.

The point is that if people don't say anything when they see something wrong happening then nothing will ever get better.

*First they came for the Communists*

*and I did not speak out –*
*because I was not a Communist.*
*Then they came for the Socialists*
*and I did not speak out –*
*because I was not a Socialist.*
*Then they came for the Trade Unionists*
*and I did not speak out –*
*because I was not a Trade Unionist.*
*Then they came for the Jews and I did not speak out -*
*because I was not a Jew.*
*Then they came for me –*
*and there was no one left to speak out for me.*

And I know someone will say, "omg this is not about NAZIS stupid sera durr" and that it is wrong to put that in the same place as this. But did you stop to wonder why it is that it is all girls on that website? It is just more oppression and people telling us how we should behave and what we should look like and if you don't look like the magazines say then you suck. Only it is us doing it to ourselves. And no one wants to be the person who says it is not OK so it just goes on and on and on.

You can all turn on me and yell at me again tomorrow but I'm trying to do the right thing by someone and if you can't see that then you can bog off back to the toilets and throw up twenty times a day for all I care.

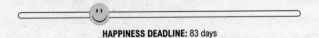

**HAPPINESS DEADLINE:** 83 days

**4.56 p.m. Tuesday 30 January** | **i'm sorry?**

Dear Person I Will Not Name,

Please will you at least talk to me? I don't care about the others and I know it isn't you making them do all this. I don't care if none of them talk to me ever again. I just want to sit down with you and give you a hug and make this OK. Which is what I should have done all along and I GET THAT NOW.

I miss you?
sera xxxx

**HAPPINESS DEADLINE:** 82 days

---

**6.56 p.m. Thursday 1 February** | **There is not really a title that fits this**

I know I should probably not even put anything on here, because it has not exactly worked out so far. Apparently this is hard for people to get their brains around but I did not actually sit down last weekend and think "Hey! What would be total wincakes would be to make my best friend cry in French and run out and not come back and for her to not speak to me or even look at me while her 'real' friends are coming at me with scissors and taking chunks out of my hair gosh yay funz."

But now my mum is getting phone calls. And like I don't really care now what you do to me but people phoning my mum and making her cry is NOT OK. Not even at all OK.

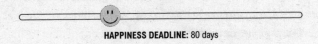

**HAPPINESS DEADLINE:** 80 days

---

2.45 p.m. Friday 2 February | **ummm**

So, er, I might be moving schools.

patchworkboy, am not answering mobile. Can't talk about it right now.

**HAPPINESS DEADLINE:** 79 days

---

11.26 p.m. Saturday 3 February | **my brain hurts**

I feel so unbelievably knackerated and I still totally can't sleep. The Monster has tried to drown me in Horlicks which was sort of kind of her (she heard me playing Ver Jointz and was all "Oh, is this your friend's band, let's chat about guitars even though I know nothing and think The Sugababes are what Teh Kids like" even though she was sort of half asleep and with her hair all bouncy and sticky uppy and wow, she looks sort of human without all that monster slap on). So I went Yawn Yawn V Tired etc and she totally wasn't buying any of it.

I feel like a total spoon. People who burst into tears in restaurants should be doing it because they have just been told by their One True Love that the One True Love can never be because he has The Cancer or some glamorous wasting disease. And there should be artful tears neatly plopping off someone's nose on to a chocolate pudding, and they should sweep off into the night together and not have to stop to pay the bill. It should not involve:

a) snot
b) parents
c) Pizza Hut

Only I was so freaked out because OMG the moving schools thing has mutated into being sent away to ~~Hogwarts~~ some nobby girls' school a million miles away where they probably make you wear kilts and OH MY GOD WTF. To punish me for getting bullied and spat at and having my PE kit pissed on, which is OBVS ALL MY OWN FAULT he wants to send me to some farking prison where I would be the freakish New Girl who knew no one and got bullied and spat at and had my PE kit pissed on only by posh kids instead. Who are probably all anorexic anyway. And I don't get to actually have a choice in this because he is the PARENT and I am not to be trusted to make good decisions for myself and I will look back and thank him when I am 93 or whatever. And I wanted to KILL HIM only I was just crying and crying.

And obviously it was all Mum's fault as well because when isn't it. And money and her not having any. So obviously I was very calm and pointed out to him that him and his Monstertart are the reason we live in the grotty bit of Carterton, and actually even if we were still living in the big old stupid house I would still be going to the same school, and how I am not leaving Mum on her own FFS so he can swan about telling people his daughter goes to private school and if he is so bothered how come he isn't saying I should come and live with him, even though if he did I would say no anyway except he won't so it doesn't matter. Only I didn't say any of those things obvs because snot cry wail.

And then he was like it is not just the school stuff, and he had a big rant about how he didn't want to be the last to know everything just because he isn't there, and it ended up being my fault then because I am obviously off having a life and doing lots of interesting new things (ker-wha?) and when I come to see him I don't really talk to him or say anything at all in fact apart from "No I would not like anchovies, blerg" etc. Which is sort of true and why I am trying to do Resolution #6: Being nicerish to Dad etc, but it is DIFFICULT. I am NOT going to moan to him about Mother because that would be awful and mean, and I feel bad enough about saying mean things about her on here when she has been all sweet and huglike and listeny about all of this. And everything else is just school crap and why would he care? I don't care about what he does at work all day. And then he went on about how he's been worrying about me for a long time because we used to be so close and have a laugh together and now I've changed and am "secretive" and "those friends of yours" are a Bad Influence. Uh, that would involve me actually HAVING some friends. Way to be on the clue bus, Daddy-O. And the Monster was all, "Maybe we could save this for another time dear" and all the waitresses were staring as I snotted all over the stuffed crusts and out-wailed the five-year-old on the next table who didn't want his ice cream.

(Memo to those parents: Er, if your kid doesn't want the ice cream, just let him not have the ice cream, dudes. It's not like it's made from seeds and berries and nutritional supplements. It is ice cream. And your kid is quite fat and toxic. He can do without, k?)

So we came back to the house and he was all, "We need to have a serious discussion, you are obviously very unhappy" and OMG how does he think that is going to fix it when it is not ME making me unhappy? And then to get him to shut up I yelled at him and told him the Cute Boffin Man had said it was his fault for being a rubbish dad (which isn't exactly true but sort of is) and then there was yet more WEEPING and WAILING and lo the heavens did open.

I still have that sick feeling of having cried too much, and my nose feels sort of tight and hot, and I'm over the hiccupy bit now (hate that bit) but I just know we'll get as far as breakfast and he'll want to TALK ABOUT IT and I feel sort of teary again just thinking about that. I don't want to TALK ABOUT IT. I want there to not be an IT to talk about. I just want to go home and for everything to be normal and to giggle with Kym and annoy old ladies on the bus and for her to do my eyeliner and go to the bandstand. Which is, um, probably never going to happen again. And now I am crying again.

The really pathetic thing is that through all of this Mum and Dad have actually been talking on the phone, and it reminded me of when I was 14 and I broke my leg, and it was not long after he moved out, and me and Mum were still in the old house, and he would come over to see me and sometimes I'd catch them laughing and I totally thought they would get back together because of me and how I'd made it happen by breaking my leg. And when they didn't, I thought maybe I should break my other leg in case they hadn't had enough time, and I spent weeks and weeks almost walking in front of cars and falling off stuff and I never managed to break my other leg and for ages I thought that if only I had broken it they would've totally got back together.

And now I don't think I would care too much if they got back together. I could tick some things off my Resolutions list, maybe, and just not have to think about them. But I don't think we would talk more and be all close and father/daughter-y if he still lived with us. I suppose it would mean I could spend all my weekends at home and not have to come here. But then I have nothing to do anyway because I have no friends. (That is not self-pity: it is in my user profile that I have been unfriended. Umm, like I hadn't got the message.) And they would fight anyway because that's what people do. Even Dad and the Monster have fights, which are of course all about me. (I bet they have other ones when I'm not here about who will cook the pasta this evening and whether she has spent too much on perfume or whatever it is that people like them fight about.) So really, it would be like now, except Dad wouldn't have to take me out somewhere and buy me a present twice a month.

Maybe the Monster and Dad should get married and then split up so I can have guilty stepmother presents too.

Erk. I am such a horrible person and I so don't care.

Sleep possibly a good idea now.

And I am still comments-disabled because this is just me rambling in the middle of the night and I don't need anyone's opinion or anything, this is just me. Although there is probably no one who will read it anyway.

**HAPPINESS DEADLINE:** 78 days *fails to LOL*

New phone! It is charging now. With proper contract and everything so I won't keep running out of credit, and when I get home/read instructions/ask patchworkboy how it works, ringtone of Jointiness!

Feel guilty now. We went out to get it right after breakfast only it's Sunday so the shop wasn't even open for another twenty minutes so we had to just sit in the car. ZOMG awkwardness. I suck at talking.

PAPA: You look lovely today darling. I especially like the way your face is massive and swollen from crying so that you resemble a small moon.

SELF: ...

PAPA: gosh what a large seagull.

SELF: ...

PAPA: ...

SELF: ...

PAPA: Um er by the way Julia thinks perhaps changing schools might be disruptive with exams etc coming up so maybe we will not do that thing that made you cry for six hours in a row in case you become even more of an embarrassing failure than you are already.

SELF: OK...

PAPA: What shall we have for lunch tum-ti-tum.

*drums hands on steering wheel*

I bet he only told me it was the Monster's idea cos he hoped it would make me go "No Daddy please let me do what YOU want" or something. But at least the kilt-wearing Posh School thing is not happening. And if I want to go to sixth-form college instead of staying in the same place next year then I could do that but only if I wanted. Which ... um. That is good, y/y?

Um.

Can I just not have to go to school at all and become a chimney sweep instead or something?

And the phone was really expensive but he was all "you should have a good one" and got me the same one he has, and Mum will think he's only doing it to make her look bad even though she won't actually say so, only he's really only doing it because I told him he was a rubbish dad yesterday. So now all of us will feel terrible. Arg. Stupid life.

Camera phone, though, woo. Prepare for mucho picspam of, I dunno, my bedroom or my feet or something.

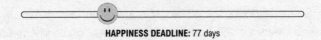

**HAPPINESS DEADLINE:** 77 days

---

7.45 p.m. Sunday 4 February | **wtf?**

So apparently the entire WORLD got together while I was at Dad's to discuss My Future and What Is Best For Everyone and OMG my mum bought those little tiny bagels and the little twirly things with smoked salmon in them which are the only reason I even know about it.

MUM: Hello darling daughter. I expect you had an awful time with Papa and his h0r.

MOI: Um yes whatever. I hate them and love you best. Why are there peanuts in a little dish in the living room?

MUM: Ummmm.

MOI: You have spent the weekend with your sekrit new boyf having noisy sex in the living room. With peanuts.

MUM: *yelps* No no no that would be Wrong. The truth

which is much less Wrong of course is that I invited all the parents of the people you have pissed off lately around to have a Group Sharing Moment about the overwhelming messed-upped-ness of you all. I read about it in my book How to Make Your Children Hate You.

MOI: Oh. Em. Gee.

Apparently I am "overemotional" and it would have been "unhelpful" to have me there. Which I proved totally wrong obvs by FLAILING and telling her I hate her more than the Monster. MATURITY FOR THE WIN!

So. I am ignoring the WTFery of my mum and Kym's mum and Sasha's parents and Naima's dad (omg where did she get all these people's phone numbers from?) sitting around in our living room eating poncy nibbles FROM M&S NOT EVEN TESCO, because it is tiny-small compared to the WTFery of the rest of it. Which is basically them saying that I made everything up due to being MENTAL and that Jaden only did the pissing thing as a JOKE and I am just too SENSITIVE and supposedly everything is all fixed and mended and we are all best best friends again and nothing even happened except inside sera's crazy broken head.

Mkay. I will remember that tomorrow when I am bouncing off some lockers.

On the plus side it appears Daddy-O kept his mouth shut about me having a weeping fit when he dropped me off so I don't have to explain all of that. Even if he's probably only doing it because he thinks it's all his fault and he wants Mum to think I only have a perfect wonderful time at his house with fairies and ponies and pink icing, what with those being the favourite things of Princess Serafina.

So anyway I have to be at school tomorrow to prove that my

mother's Magical Nibbles have sorted everything. Just in case anyone wants to prepare the knives, guns, bombs etc. If you could not go for my hair again that would be handy though, cos Della came down and spent like an hour trying to make it look less carp.

Comments are ~~gay~~ ~~German~~ disabled (cos, you know, I haven't offended anyone for a whole ten minutes) but I am not Whispering things. This whole thing happened because of people not being truthful and honest and trying to hide things and that is not what I am here for.

UPDATED: Shag, forgot to say: patch, I forgot my old phone so I didn't get your texts all weekend and I was too chicken to look at my emails but THANK YOU and I'm sorry and I will totally understand if you want to run away from the crazy girl with the messed-up life etc. :D

UPDATED: OMG Dad keeps phoning me up. Dude, I just spent a whole weekend at your house with you talking at me: whatever you want to say is probably covered. Seriously, like, *three* missed calls? Chillax.

**HAPPINESS DEADLINE:** 77 days

---

4.34 p.m. Monday 5 February | **stfu paris hilton**

OMG I am like famous. And now for something apart from The Incident. Put me in Heat magazine, pplz!

Officially Weirdest. Day. Ever. Like, possibly there were some lessons, but really everyone was just talking about the Thing and how Kym wasn't in school STILL. And then her mum came to see Mr Fletcher at first break, and I was sort of terrified, and then I got called in to see Mr Fletcher and got even more terrified, and had to stand outside his office with my feet going all pinsy-needly and with Miss Kosminski and everyone going past and just sort of nodding at me and not smiling and argh. And I can't say what he said because he asked me not to talk about it, and he was all non-horrible to me so I won't. But I think everyone kind of knows what is going on anyway.

I was going to just go home at lunch time because OMG EXHAUSTED, but then really unexpected people were like amazingly kind and nice to me, and sat with me at lunch so I was not all lonesome and friendless, and then sat with me in Science as well so I was not lonesome or friendless or completely confused by electrons either (yay!). Which is all a bit guiltmaking and strange, because, erm, complicated. And I still feel sort of awful about everything. But also quite wooful too.

Oh, and Resolution #8: Become less pathetically single? :D I am officially boyfriended.

See? Weirdest. Day. Ever.

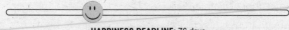

**HAPPINESS DEADLINE:** 76 days

COMMENTS

**frantastica**

Hiya honey! Hope I wasn't one of the guilt-involving people! There was an entire assembly about you. You really are famous!

### serafina67

I know! She was like, "Here is a story about Secrets and Friendship and Responsibility" and then it was like SUBTEXT whoa! And everyone stared at me and I went all red and just kind of hid under my still-quite-wonky hair.

*wibbles* Maybe there was a bit of guilt-involvingness? But only because I have been sort of a betch. To, like, EVERYONE. But maybe especially to you. I still feel really bad about the NYE party, and letting Kym say mean things without, like, disagreeing or whatever. I am just the worst friend evah pls to be knowing that? But then you sort of know that already. :(

Also: *waves hello to Francesca the noob*

### frantastica

Oi, I'm not a noob! I was on here before everyone else, I just didn't ever tell you my ULife name. I'm not angry any more, though, honestly. Sometimes people fall out: it doesn't have to be anyone's fault. If anyone should feel guilty it's probably me! Don't read through any of my old posts from last year, OK, sweetie? I don't think I was very understanding about what you were going through.

Oh, and in case anyone else tells you: in Drama we did role plays about confidentiality and sources of help if someone was "in trouble". *So* subtle!

### serafina67

OMG, I had like no idea you were into net stuff. You are like the All New Francesca who I don't even know.

*hugs on you*

Urk, your Drama class all hate me.

### frantastica

They don't all hate you, hon: they hate "Alfonso", who told

"Mr Patel" that "Sami" stole a Mars Bar. I do love how when they're trying to be ultra-PC they still have Mr Patel running a corner shop. *facepalm*

*hugs you back* Of course, friends again! I have to get to know the All New Serafina too.

**patchworkboy**

Return of the comments! Huzzah! Please don't do that again: it makes me worry about you.

"Official"? This is the "date" business all over again, isn't it? I can see I'm going to have to be very precise from now on. *prints out certificate with "ILU" on it*

**serafina67**

LOL, sorry, I just meant like now people know and everything. Certificate, awww. We are the officialest!

*prints out voucher for snogs four times a week*

No more disableds! And it was sweet of you to worry but I was obviously not swinging from my daddy's ceiling fan all weekend or I would not have been posting. And you should've seen the spam in my inbox from all the forum trolls etc so I kind of had to or I would've drowned under all the TYPING OF EVOL!!!!1!1

Soz I had to come straight home but I promised Mum I would and I am soooo tired.

**patchworkboy**

*hangs about Like a groupie hoping for a smile*

Seriously, if you disappear off and your mobile is off and you're offline for ages, people worry. Just sayin', for future reference and all.

**serafina67**

Heh, no panic, I'm not that emo.

OOH, love that song:

*sings along*

*Hoping for a smile, waiting for her turn, just a little while:
VERY little while …* ;D

**patchworkboy**

Gig Saturday?

**serafina67**

Darling must check my very busy diary, might be having tea
with Queen, Natalie Portman, etc.

*has it written on calendar in purple pen with stars round it*
*is dorky*

**patchworkboy**

Congrats: officially least emo calendar in history.

**serafina67**

It is a Godbotherer calendar so, um, yes.
*facepalm*

**patchworkboy**

*grins*

See how you have grown as an individual since you met
me.

**serafina67**

Morrissey for TEH WIN!

**cameraobscurer**

Friended you, hope that's OK.

**serafina67**

Whee, hello Cam! Friends = coolness. Love your ULife (pix
of Joints, well, duh!).

**georgia_darkly**

Just wanted to say I thought what you did was awesome
and that girl is better off now.

**serafina67**

TY! Do I know you?

**georgia_darkly**

Nope, I am in Pittsburgh, PA. Was just googling anorexia+mermaids and your thing came up and I just kind of got reading.

**serafina67**

Woo, I am like global!

Anorexia + mermaids???

**georgia_darkly**

What can I tell ya, I have eclectic tastes.

**8utterflywings**

Hi, here from georgia_darkly's. And, uh, what she said. (About your friend, not about mermaids. IDK what the hell that's all about.)

**Serafina67**

OMG my fame is unstoppable! MOAR INTERNET FRIENDS YAY!

**daisy13**

I'm really glad things are better now. I hope your friend gets some help like you wanted. You must be a really good person to have tried to help her like that.

**serafina67**

Aww, thx. I feel kind of messed up about it still and keep thinking of things to text her about and then going "Oh". :(

But she is getting help now, yes. There is some sort of special centre or something where she can go to school and have therapies and things and her mum is taking her next week. I bet they have insanely evil rules and she will hate it. And me. But it is better that than things staying the same, I suppose.

Where do you live? I keep forgetting people can read this from like Australia and America and wherever.

**daisy13**

Didn't you say before you were in Carterton? Not far from you, actually!! But I'm not supposed to give out my info online except to people I trust.

**serafina67**

Ha ha, me too, oops. My parents are the King and Queen of Strictness. Except about all the things they don't know about, heh.

**daisy13**

The less they know the better?

**Serafina67**

Yeppers. ;)

Are you really 13? I looked at your profile and I can't tell! And you don't have anything in your blog. :( I added you to my friends anyway, hope that's OK.

**daisy13**

I don't really keep a diary. But I like reading yours and talking to you!! I think you can get really close to someone that way.

And no, I'm not really 13 ;)

**serafina67**

Haha, I am not exactly 67 either. This place is filled with LIARZ!

---

6.20 p.m. Thursday 8 February | **tap tap tap**

OK, am engaging Official Action Plan of actually getting off my arse and doing things for the Happiness Deadline. Mainly because

I am seeing Crazy Pete again on Sat and he is big into me being "proactive" and such. And also because I am feeling much less terrible and totally loved-up awwww and slightly as if I might be able to get my carp together by April 22nd after all.

So far this week I have:

- become surgically attached to patchworkboy
- comment-spammed lovely new internet friends (shush this was just as important as homework if not more, k?)
- made Mum laugh by cooking World's Most Lumpy Mashed Potato with her
- phoned up Dad and Done Talking with him
- even asked if the Monster was there so I could talk to her too (which she wasn't yay but I get points for trying yes?)
- entirely avoided having an Incident over the whole lolbabe thing which is like miraculous
- missed her a bit though (this is me being Completely Totally Honest)

GO TEAM SERA!

Obvs I am still completely failing at thinness but pff. *eats crisp, does not care*

And even though it is not on the list me and frantastica are going to work on a VTN together, because she is Brainy And Dedicated and I am Idea-Filled But Skippy and never finish things. Woo! And we were very bored in Skience today and so made notes and drew the hair of the heroines and now I have stuck them over my desk so as to be inspired. But it is sekrit so SHUSH.

frantastica has a VTN of her own that she has been working on for aaages and is like 21,000 words or something omg. But it is sekrit too so DOUBLE-SHUSH.

And I am still going to write Joe Meo and Rue Liette (star-crossed lovers, she is a French waitress in a café in 1900, he plays the guitar in the same café in the present, there is a time portal that opens every time anyone makes coffee, word count: 82) only I will do that one on my own because it is sort of insane.

Yay! *types like a mo-fo*

**HAPPINESS DEADLINE:** 73 days

COMMENTS

**frantastica**
It's not very secret if you tell everyone!

**serafina67**
Oops soz!

**frantastica**
That's OK, hon!
I'm not confident like you about writing, that's all. I wouldn't want people to read it unless it was good enough, and it might never be that.

**serafina67**
LOL confident? More like aware of my own craptasticness so not worrying about it.
Also I have this mental thing where I sort of divide up real life and ULife, even though they are connected, so it feels like it is serafina who is the one doing the writing? And serafina is WAY more confident than Sarah.
Um. I make no sense and am schizo.

**patchworkboy**

So which one of you am I going out with?

**serafina67**

Serafina, definitely. :D

**georgia darkly**

Is VTN some Brit thing?

**serafina67**

Hee, no, it is just a me thing. It means Very Thrilling Novel. Which is sort of optimistic all round. Maybe I should change it to EAB: Embarrassing Abandoned Beginnings cos that is all I have so far.

**georgia darkly**

Yeah, 82 words is kinda short for a novel. :-P

---

6.46 p.m. Friday 9 February | **woe is me**

OK, it sucks being a Guitar Widow. I am sitting here lonely by the telephone while Patch noodles with his Jointy palz far far away. GIGS ARE IMPORTANT BUT GFS ARE MORE SO, K?

See how subtle that was. I am learning Girlfriendese.

Also: does anyone know anything about graphs? Because I am supposed to be marking asymptotes in red on this bit of paper and that would involve me knowing what they are. And having a red pen. (Yes, I am doing maths homework on a Friday night. This is because I am ~~a huge nerd~~ ~~very slightly in the poo about my mocks results and trying to stop Mum stressing~~ mature and organized.)

*apologizes to lovely new blogfriends who really aren't interested in maths*

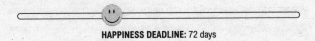

**HAPPINESS DEADLINE:** 72 days

COMMENTS

**cameraobscurer**

He's not noodling. It is ART, dude.

**serafina67**

Mhmm yuhuh OK. If you are doing Important Band Things why are you online?

**cameraobscurer**

Because ~~Rishy~~ someone forgot the extension lead so we are all sitting here like lemony things waiting about? It is the Krazee World of Rock!

**serafina67**

Then omg kick Patch out and tell him to come here? He will know about the maths for one thing.

**frantastica**

Do you want me to email you the maths solutions? I would explain it, but it really requires hand gestures and so on: not so good for the online.

**serafina67**

Awesomeness! Or you could come over? Mother is upstairs getting wonkfaced on chardonnay with Della and I am loooooooooonely.

**frantastica**

Sorry, sweetie! It's a bit late for Dad to drive me anyway, and it sounds like your mum couldn't give me a lift back.

**serafina67**

Grr. One day we will all have cars and will be able to go wherever we want. Or they will invent magical teleporters which will allow us to press a button on a wristwatch and POOF we shall be there where we want to be in an instant. Or something.

Bet the teleporters will be invented sooner than all of us having cars.

**patchworkboy**

*hops in his TARDIS and materializes in sera's room*

**serafina67**

OMG YOU ARE DOCTOR WHO!! I love you!

**patchworkboy**

*flirts Doctorishly and shows you planets, monsters, etc*

**serafina67**

Whee! I am all companiony!

(Um, this is lovely, but WHY ARE YOU ONLINE NOT AT BAND PRACTICE THING?)

**patchworkboy**

Sorry: Rishy was just setting up the lead and Cam said you were bored.

**serafina67**

I am sacking you and running off with the Doctor. So ner.

**patchworkboy**

*laments*

**serafina67**

*is far away on Raxacoricofallapatorious and cannot hear the lamenting*

**serafina67**

HELLO? BF? You are supposed to chase after me and have

a big fight with the Doctor over who loves me most and maybe step on his sonic screwdriver to prove how much you win and he is only a man with a magic pentorch.

### daisy13

You and your boyfriend are really sweet. I guessed you two were going to get together ages ago.

So your mum lets him come round when she isn't there? You're lucky.

### serafina67

What the old dear doesn't know... ;)

She is still at the "Now young man what are your intentions towards my darling daughter and what is that haircut all about anyway?" stage, so there is to be No Going Into The Bedroom or any of that business. Haha poor deluded woman. It is sad to think that at her age she believes naughty rude things can only happen in a bedroom. I think maybe she should get out more, apart from that obviously involving mothersex, EW.

*scrubs eyes with soap, etc*

OMG, you have been paying way too much attention! What I write in here is mostly all incomprehensible faff and prolly TMI. Why anyone else would give a toss I have no clue.

### daisy13

Parents are useless at noticing things, aren't they?

TMI?

Sorry, I hope I didn't seem weird asking about your boyfriend!!

### serafina67

LOL, no problemo. I'm sort of flattered. Child of Divorce = Giant Attention Ho.

TMI = Too Much Information.

**daisy13**

:)

OK!! Glad I didn't upset you. You seem like a lovely person. Some people on the internet seem to make a lot of things up about themselves, but you seem really genuine.

**serafina67**

Complete and Total Honesty, bitchez!

**daisy13**

And I really like hearing about your boyfriend. He seems like a nice guy. Is he older than you?

**serafina67**

Yes but only a bit. I have known him since I was a tiny child, which is sort of terrifying and strange actually. My mum has a photo somewhere of us dressed up as the Innkeeper and the Innkeeper's Wife in the Christmas play. We are holding hands and everything. It is like destiny OMG!

**patchworkboy**

You have changed a little since that photograph was taken.

**serafina67**

Um, yes? I have, like, teeth now. (Prolly same height though, grr.)

You have changed a bit too. The Innkeeper does not have big FO boots and stubbliness and that little wisp of hair over his ear that is ever so slightly curly and even though he tucks it out of the way it sneaks out to say hello and makes me want to wrap it round my little finger.

**patchworkboy**

OK, am coming over now.

**serafina67**

*squees*

OMG Mother it is like sleeping time please to not be waking me up to talk to me about sex? Because OMG SHUSH.

Yes, it is nearly Valentine's Day and your freakish daughter has somehow managed to be boyfriended. And yes we were in a sort of person-knot on the sofa when you came in yesterday and ZOMG EMBARRASSING. But, um, there are some things that I just do not need to be having conversations about, k?

And before anyone goes "Durrr sera what happened to Complete Total Honesty on your ULife?", um, no. Just because Tamlyn Robinson gives anyone who steps into the girls' loos a blow-by-blow account (YES INDEED) with sound effects and mime of every single incident in her and Kai Soper's, um, ACTIVITIES, does not mean I am going to. There are some things that I don't need to share. Especially not with like the entire internet.

And YES WOMAN I KNOW ABOUT CONDOMS etc, omg. *eyerolls*

She is taking me shopping for frock suitable for Valentine's Day Exciting Date (hint hint at patchworkboy: we are having one of those, yes?) after I see Crazy Pete though, so she is win really. *huggles on her*

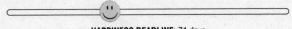

**HAPPINESS DEADLINE:** 71 days

COMMENTS

**patchworkboy**
Shame. I was so looking forward to reading all about your sex life.

**serafina67**

Exactly! I mean ... argh. I can't say what I mean! We have broken the internet!

**o jon o**

So does that mean you are or you aren't?

**patchworkboy**

And the prize for missing the point goes to ...

---

5.14 p.m. Saturday 10 February | **ummm**

So I went to see Peter the Funky Therapist all squeeful because omg SO much to say.

I totally wanted to tell him all about the thing with Kym so he could go Yes Sera Well Done You and about the whole Moving Schools/Not Moving Schools trauma and how everything was cool and I am happier now because my friends aren't actually total bitchez and I have a patchworkboy and am actually doing lots of the Resolutiony things already and am SO going to make the deadline and yay. And HELLO THERAPIST MAN I AM SUPPOSED TO DO THE TALKING, DUDE.

ME:                  I tried to do a good thing for someone and even though it backfired liek whoa and nearly got me stabbed with scissors and was probably actually stupid in the first place it was still meant to be a good thing.

CRAZY PETE:    I think this is a sign you still have body-image issues.

ME:                  No you are confusing me with the other person.

The other person has MENTAL ILLNESSES over what she looks like. Score to me!

CRAZY PETE: Do you think this is because your parents got divorced?

ME: Ummm wtf? We are talking about someone else's eating disorders.

CRAZY PETE: STFU betch! I know best what with me being the therapist man and you being only at school. Now let us talk about The Incident. Again. Because you are clearly heading for another one of those even though you are stupid and think you are quite happy at the moment. YOU ARE WRONG!

ME: Um yes sir.

And I wanted to tell him about ULife, and how even though sometimes it is a bit madcakes I have met people like 8utterflywings and georgia_darkly and daisy13 and it is mostly just very yay to have people reading what you have written and commenting back because it makes you feel like people are actually listening to you for once in your whole stupid crappy life, only HE WAS NOT LISTENING TO ME LONG ENOUGH FOR ME TO SAY SO.

It would be funny if it did not make me FILLED WITH RAGE and WANTING TO SHOUT IN CAPSLOCK.

Well, it is a bit funny.

And I don't care anyway because LESS THAN FIVE hours till Ver Jointeez are onstage. Woo! Plus Mummy took her flat squished daughter out afterwards and desquishified her by finding perfect Valentinable outfit. OMG PRETTY.

Oh and I am going to do something "interesting" with my hair with the aid of the fantastical frantastica who is coming over like NOW. I have gone all girlified, lolz.

11.56 p.m. Saturday 10 February | **ten reasons why tonight was the best night ever in the history of ever**

1) OMG it was a Joints gig. Like duh. They are the Best. Band. Ever. And it was a proper proper gig in a proper venue in town and yay.

2) OMG I am now a raven-haired temptress thanks to frantastica and the nice people at L'Oreal who make the black goo. And someone who I had never met before told me I looked "pale and interesting" and someone else threatened to bottle me for being a Goth. If only I could be bothered with having to start again on the wardrobe ~~and if Kym was still here to do my eyeliner~~ I would be so there.

3) frantastica also managed to not dye the bathroom black like I did that time before, which was Unpopular. Although she did dye parts of herself black, which was very noble and friend-like of her what with it being the primo pulling opportunity of the year.

4) patchworkboy struck poses like a God of Rock. BECAUSE HE IS ONE OMGYES.

5) I may have got just a leetle bit dwunk. But only a leetle bit cos look, no typos! Jober as a sudge, yr honour. And also beer = a bit yucky.

6) I may have also bought some faglets from the shop without

being asked for ID because of my amazingly age-creating raven-haired hairiness. And then nearly set fire to the raven-haired hairiness in a fit of enthusiasm. And then given them to some random bloke because faglets = yuckier than beer actually.

7) Did I mention that patchworkboy was, er, quite good? (And obviously cameraobscurer too. And all of them. But I was a bit distracted.)

8) Sasha was there even though she always said she does not do Unders gigs except as a favour for friends or to pull and she was a complete Billy No-Mates. Plus also ummm you are at a Jointz gig in three-inch heels and a little tiny belt of a skirt with no tights on so you cannot dance or do anything except stand in the corner with face like slapped arse? WHY ARE YOU HERE?

9) frantastica spent all night being stared at by Pretty Man Who She Likes and is totally in there. :D

AND SAVING THE BEST TILL LAST:

10)OMG THEY PLAYED "GROUPIE" AND CAM DEDICATED IT TO "THE GIRL WHO KNOWS ALL THE WORDS BETTER THAN I DO, SHE KNOWS WHO SHE IS".

*flails*

*collapses*

*dies completely*

I keep typing things and deleting them to try to explain how amazing that was. It is all just dorky things about feeling SPESHUL which makes me sound like some kind of person with Needs who has to wear a name label and an orange baseball cap when I go out so people can find me if I get lost. But it did make me feel special, in a not-retarded-person way. Like it was just for me even though there was a roomful of other people there. And now I don't want to play that song on the CD because I don't want to spoil remembering what it sounded like tonight, and I know that really does sound borderline mentalist but I know what I mean.

I wish you could put these things in bottles and keep them for ever and ever, and whenever you wanted you could just open the bottle and sniff it and it would send you back to exactly how it was the first time, not like a memory or a pic or what you said about it later but actually being there for real and it happening all over again. Heaven heaven heaven.

Hee, Mum just came in and was supposed to be telling me off for being up on the lappytoppy so late, but she was too busy being cute about my hair (which she LIKES omg) and me being so bouncy and happy and she has NO idea about the booze'n'fags (I have been to a nite-club Mother this is why I smell of ashtrays and bingo, no rly, omg you are buying that? Win!). I think actually this is not simply me being a ~~Master~~ Mistress of Disguise but because she was also out on the razz herself (work drinks on a Saturday? Whatevs) and got in about half an hour later than I did so cannot bitch at me. I suspect she has been off doing Teh Rude with someone but don't want to ask in case she hasn't and then gets upset because she has no one to do Teh Rude with. And also, ew. Parents, eh?

Pff, don't want to go to sleep. Gonna go spam some forums or something.

UPDATED: Wow the GB forum is full of retardz these days.

UPDATED: Sasha is STILL bitching about me on her ULife. Er, wha? Ancient History. I have moved on. You need to move on too. And maybe not lie about me online quite so much, k? Though she only has two friends listed in her profile so no one will read it anyway. ~~I am not unattractively smug about this no not me honest~~. Also for someone who was supposed to be very concerned about

A Certain Person, she is kind of amazingly offensive about her when she thinks no one is looking, omg.

UPDATED: OMG I just spent half an hour playing a Neighbours game where Harold Bishop throws hot dogs at you. Errr GO TO BED WOMAN?

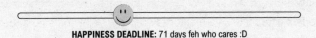

**HAPPINESS DEADLINE:** 71 days feh who cares :D

COMMENTS

**georgia darkly**

OK, you little Britchiks have way better social lives than we did.

**serafina67**

OMG no this was like the first time EVER I went to a thing like this! Usually it is all OMG school exams stayathomestaringatceiling, only I try not to mention those bits as they are quite lametastic. :(

**georgia darkly**

Quit stealing MY teenage experience, dude!

**frantastica**

That was quite the evening! I still have purple arms, though.

**serafina67**

OMG sorry! I have weird stains on my neck and one black ear like a dinky little puppy, but otherwise am mysteriously uncovered in goo. I will hire you again hairdressing lady! You seemed to be enjoying yourself ~~what with having your face snogged off by a nice young man~~. ;)

**frantastica**

Ahem. I behaved in a perfectly delicate and ladylike way

while I was having my face snogged off.

(By the way, he's not on here, but Lex is, so thank you for
Subtle Anonymity.)

**serafina67**

*is possibly hungover or something*

wtf?

**frantastica**

Never mind! Will explain tomorrow.

**serafina67**

Come over?

**frantastica**

Violin practice, homework, dog walking etc. Sundays =
dullness chez moi.

**patchworkboy**

*pats the dinky little puppy*

**serafina67**

Hee! Did I say enough nice things about you, sweetie?

**patchworkboy**

Not bad. ;)

Although the sound was rough as rats and Jono totally
bolloxed up the intro on "Adrenaline Ride".

Sorry I didn't walk you home. Rishy's dad had to get all the
gear into his car straight after because the manager of the
Bunker was being an arse so I couldn't hang about.

Less of the "sweetie": I have Important Rock Cred to
maintain.

**serafina67**

I shall just drop to my knees and worship every time I see
you then.

No bother about the getting home thing, knew you were
busy and I am not Psycho GF dangling from your elbow

(although obvs according to Mother Dearest you walked me home safe and sound because that is the kind of responsible considerate person you are and are therefore trustworthy enough to come round when she is not here to knock on the door every five minutes with stupid I-am-checking-for-shagging-teenagers excuses).

And don't lie, you were Teh Awesome!

**patchworkboy**

*I shall just drop to my knees and worship every time I see you then.*

*waggles eyebrows*

**serafina67**

OMG I AM A GREAT BIG HO PLEASE INFORM EVERYONE.

**patchworkboy**

Nonsense. You are perfectly in proportion.

**serafina67**

I wish. :(

**patchworkboy**

Shush. *hugs*

**daisy13**

That sounds like a really cool weekend!!

Your hair sounds amazing. I'd love to see it.

**serafina67**

Haha, was ROCKIN wknd though now I have brain-ache and bleh school. Waaah why not half-term yet?

Would show you the Amazing Hair but am too stoopid to work out how to get pics off my phone and on to the internets. Sigh. Am amazed Mum didn't freak out over hair as I have dyed my pillow a bit grey and look like a zombie, which is the sort of the thing the neighbours don't like. Well, she thinks so anyway. So she is in the good books.

Have you ever dyed your hair?

**daisy13**

I've never dyed my hair. :)

That's a shame about your phone. I bet you look really grown up and glamorous.

**serafina67**

omg you should. It is so funny. I keep walking past myself in mirrors and going "Um, who is that??" Mum says I look like a bohemian (wtf?) which made me think of that weird song with all the funny voices on it and the bit about dancing a fandango. It is anciently old but we used to play it in the car when I was little. Sooooo cheesy.

**daisy13**

Bohemian Rhapsody by Queen?

**serafina67**

OMG YES!

**daisy13**

It's a classic song. I'm listening to it now.

**serafina67**

Lolz, classic yes. Where classic = ooooooooooooold. Though I am into loads of old stuff now like Nirvana. Retro Emo for the win!

Soz if spelling wonky, am kernackered. :)

92

Sample of today:

> MISS CARTER: Good morning class today we shall be discussing important and exciting issues such as King Henry the Something and Stuff That He Did. Everyone now turn to page OMIGOD SERA WTF?
>
> GOTH-SERA: Umm, yes?
>
> MISS CARTER: *blinks*
>
> ENTIRE ROOMFUL OF PEOPLE: Er, Miss?
>
> MISS CARTER: *stares*
>
> GOTH-SERA: *stares back*
>
> MISS CARTER: Ahem. Yes. Kings etc.

General thumbs-uppage in school, anyway, woo. Including Mr Davies Chemistry who said, "Wow, I'm loving the hair", which I think he should maybe be arrested for.

Am now ~~watching EastEnders~~ working very hard on skience homework. Mmm, diagrams.

**HAPPINESS DEADLINE:** 69 days

COMMENTS

**frantastica**

You Know Who says you look fabulous, darlink. ;)

**serafina67**

OMG Voldemort has been eyeing me up?

**frantastica**

Well, you are looking a little bit Slytherin now. Tom Felton will not be able to resist.

**serafina67**

Eeeee sekrit crush! Why are evil people always the prettiest?

**patchworkboy**

MWAHAHAHAHAHA!

*twirls moustache evilly*

**serafina67**

OMG it is like PROFF! lolz

**patchworkboy**

*hands sera the speelchucker*

**serafina67**

*hits patch with it*

**patchworkboy**

Half-term? I think Rishy needs to book stuff.

**serafina67**

Am waiting till tomorrow when she will be more likely to say, "Yes daughter dearest of course you can." She got back from work late AGAIN and I was supposed to cook tea only I didn't because she was late so I just had some toast and apparently that was WRONG. If I ask her tonight she is going to say, "omg what *now*, bitchlet?" before I even get the words out of my mouth. Crossing fingers, toes, eyes ...

---

11.09 p.m. Tuesday 13 February | **PARTAY!**

LITTLE ME: Oh sweet and nice mother-person who I love lots

and lots: may I go on a school trip that isn't, making me be Out of Your Hair for half-term and not even eating all the cheese in the fridge like I may possibly have done earlier? There will be walks in the fresh air and it will be good for my social skills. In fact it is practically an educational trip and there will probably be an exam at the end with certificates and an awards ceremony and I will be able to put it on my university application form that will exist one day because obviously I am that clever, so really I should go for my own health and future, can I can I please?

MOTHER: Yes.

Have been slightly economical about who is going. And it being called The Dirty Weekend. But still, woo!

Also: patchworkboy has PLANS for tomorrow. And I do not know what they are. I am like one of those girls on telly who has an exciting Valentiny date to go on and everything. It's like Prom or something. Zomg I am an American!

**HAPPINESS DEADLINE:** 68 days

COMMENTS

**patchworkboy**
Sunday–Wednesday = Dirty Midweek?
*Elvis voice*
Nothing Valen-*tiny* about it, baby.
*/Elvis voice*

**serafina67**
*squees*

OK, I am definitely not telling her the Dirty part. ;D

Lalala, we're going to the beach!

**cameraobscurer**

Pack your woolly bikini: Devon = freezing in Feb.

**serafina67**

*~~cares~~*

---

5.19 p.m. Wednesday 14 February | **FARK**

Um. Looks like I should unpack the woolly bikini after all.

Parents? Are. The. SuXXor.

And patchworkboy is not answering his mobile. HELLO? CAN YOUR DAD PICK ME UP OR SOMETHING? Have just had raging screaming bitchfight with the maternal and told her my life would be entirely perfect if I never ever had to speak to her again. This will be a bit ruined if I have to slink downstairs and ask her for a lift to your house.

**HAPPINESS DEADLINE:** 67 days

COMMENTS

**frantastica**

What happened, hon? Did she just change her mind? And you were so happy today. :(

We can still hang out, two little losers together?

**serafina67**

Dad flipped out because it is his weekend and I don't normally get back till Sunday afternoon. Even though me and Mum both thought I wasn't going because he is in the middle of moving and apparently everything he owns is in boxes. And now he has suddenly pulled some magic holiday out of his arse that he supposedly has been planning forever while decorators do stuff to the new house. Even though he obviously just made it up ten minutes ago so I can't go to the thing. And he thinks I'm going to be all "Thankyouthankyou mmmholiday withparentandhisgf" too. Um, ta. Oh, and soz about Stupid Boy. Does he not know what day it is or something? :(

**frantastica**

Thank you, sweetie! I'm all right, Cath is plying me with terrible romcoms and promising to set me up with someone from her college next week (who sounds foul, but I don't want to seem ungrateful).

Can't your mum tell him you already have plans? (I am being utterly selfish here, of course.)

**serafina67**

Yay sisters! I need one of them, we could take it in turns to have to do Dad-duty.

I don't know what's going on, I think Dad gave her a hard time about saying I could go without checking with him, cos she started asking all these questions about who was driving and how many people and if "that Patrick boy" was going and I tried to be fudgy but I am a sucky liar. So now she says she wouldn't let me go even if I wasn't going away with Dad.

I dunno, maybe she only said I could go because she knew what he was planning and wanted to piss him off. If I was her and wanted to piss him off that's what I would do. They are so bloody stabby with each other on the phone. Well, I am guessing they are anyway, because she goes all teary and hangs up about two minutes after he calls so there is probably yelling and such. And then I end up shouting at her because he isn't here for me to shout at. :(

*would rather be here with you, honest*

OK, have to run and make self look fabulous and less covered in mascara-tears.

### frantastica

At least you can spend some time with your dad. Which you might not really want to do, I know, but for Resolutions etc. You always look fabulous, sweetie. *hugs*

---

8.37 p.m. Wednesday 14 February | **happy valentine's day**

A PERFECT STARRY STARRY NIGHT AT THE BUS STOP. ENTER SERA, DRESSED IN FABULOUS FROCK WITH BIG STICKY OUT SKIRT. IT MAKES HER LOOK DIVINE, PEOPLE. HEADS TURN. MEN FAINT. WOMEN FAINT TOO. SMALL ANIMALS AND MAYBE BIRDS ARE FALLING OUT OF TREES. IT IS THAT GOOD A DRESS.

SERA: Tra-la-la. What a dream. No longer must I stay at home, eating cheap yellow ice cream (grr tightarse mother) while all the other girls get taken to the drive-in. I am the luckiest girl in the world!

SERA TWIRLS AROUND FOR A BIT WHILE TWINKLY MUSIC PLAYS. SERA TWIRLS AROUND SOME MORE.

SIXTEEN BUSES GO PAST.

ALL THE PEOPLE WHO HAVE FAINTED GET UP. GRUMPY SQUIRRELS THROW NUTS.

A MOBILE PHONE RINGS.

PATCH: Ummmm. Mumble. Excuses. Blabbity-blah.

SERA: *censored in case small children pass by*

SERA SITS DOWN. A BIRD POOS ON HER DRESS. NOW SHE CANNOT EVEN TAKE IT BACK TO TOPSHOP.

END.

No comments required. Me and some yellow ice cream are far too busy to talk to you.

**HAPPINESS DEADLINE:** 67 days OMG

---

10.19 p.m. Wednesday 14 February | **awww**

OK, forgiven. That was totally adorkable. (Even if the neighbours think you are a nutter now.)

**HAPPINESS DEADLINE:** 67 days

COMMENTS

**patchworkboy**
*still guilty*

**serafina67**

Are you like double-grounded now?

**patchworkboy**

No idea. Think Dad is too busy tearing into Mum for driving me to yours to remember it was me he was pissed off with. Have left them to bite bits out of each other till he does. Happy happy funtime.

**serafina67**

Yay for your mum. Not yay for biting. *is guilty*

**patchworkboy**

*outguilts you*

**serafina67**

*guilts even harder*

**patchworkboy**

GUILTASPLOSION!

**serafina67**

ZOMG!

**cameraobscurer**

Lucky I read this one first or patchworkboy would have got a rocket up his botty. Sure he doesn't still need one?

**serafina67**

Nah, wasn't his fault. Also: standing outside my bedroom window singing Song For Witches = forgivingness.
Still pissed off about bird poo though.

**cameraobscurer**

Dude, he is SUCH a girl.
Sure you looked ace anyway, bay-bay. *offers gratis comfort snog*

**serafina67**

lolz

**daisy13**

I'm really sorry you didn't get a proper Valentine's Day. *bunch of roses* I bet you looked beautiful in your dress. I wish I could put my arms around you and give you a REAL hug.

**serafina67**

Mkay thx?

**daisy13**

I really mean it.

---

5.28 p.m. Friday 16 February | **happy camper**

I have decided after long ~~snogs~~ discussion with patchworkboy that I am going to be Very Mature about Spain.

I am sending princess!sera along on holiday who will be charming/lovely/very filled with Resolutions and happiness-finding.

This means I am leaving behind witch!serafina, who is grumpy at Monsters/dads/everything and also is just about small enough to fit in Patch's pocket and go to Devon. He will look after her till I get back and maybe make her less grumpy.

SHUSH. It makes sense if you are in my head, k?

**HAPPINESS DEADLINE:** 65 days

COMMENTS

**8utterflywings**

You and your boy are adorkable.

**serafina67**

Hee!

**frantastica**

Are there no other yous left to look after me?

**serafina67**

Um. You can have tiny!invisible!sera who sits on your shoulder while you are playing the violin and sings along a bit tunelessly? I am not sure I need her this week. :P

**frantastica**

Hurray! *inserts her into the VTN*

**serafina67**

*squees*

---

8.42 a.m. Saturday 17 February | **badgers**

OK, so they will be here to pick me up in like twenty minutes and I have wet hair and have not quite packed yet. Erm. Know it is crazy early for anyone to be around but does anyone know if I'll be able to use wifi in Spain?

UPDATED: Nm. Mum just LAUGHED at me for wanting to take the laptop on holiday. And then laughed even more cos I nearly cried. OMG like nearly a week without the internets. I will go crazy bonkers in no time at all.

Have fun without me, internets! *kisses*

6.23 p.m. Sunday 18 February | **i am in foreign!**

Haha, found internet thing at hotel and am saved! Well not really because you have to put euros in a slot and I only have two but still, woo!

I should say things about Spain but we only got here yesterday and I ate something weird with fish in it last night and spent all morning vomming. So much for not puking at mention of Monster cos I got sick on her shoe (not even on purpose, woes).

Apols for TMI but that really is all that has happened.

Obvs vom has kind of got in the way of princess!sera being lovely magic daughter but I am trying. Our rooms have a connecting door and the Monster keeps suddenly appearing through it without knocking and I have not even gone "OMG WTF GO AWAY" at her or anything. And she was nice to me when I was throwing up and held my hair out of the way and everything, so she has quite earned niceness back. We spent this afternoon lying on my bed looking at magazines with wallpaper and sofas in for their Posh New House. We are going to choose some cushions and things tomorrow for the guest room which is sort of going to be my room for when I visit, which will prolly mean me going "um yes ok?" at whatever she picks because I don't know very much about cushions etc. And we are going shopping at the beginning of March for wedding clothes for me. Argh. It is still quite tricky to like her. Due to her being, you know, EVIL.

I have failed a bit on Talking to Dad because he has spent all day pretending to be very interested in cathedrals all of a sudden. Why do people on holiday do that? You do not spend hours telling me about the finest architrave (sp?) you have ever seen when you are at home, Father Man. No need to start now.

Arg there is a little counter thing and it says I only have 1 minute left! Umm that was a waste of two euros. Sorry. ;)

**HAPPINESS DEADLINE:** 63 days

COMMENTS

**<u>frantastica</u>**
Get well soon, honey!

---

3.44 p.m. Wednesday 21 February | **baaaaaaaaaaaaaack**

*falls upon laptop*
   *hugs it madly*
   I am now:
   a)  not brown (brr, Spain = cold!)
   b)  quite tired
   c)  full of weird gloppy hot chocolate

Spain was nice and all but not home, if that makes sense. There was no nice patchworkboy to snuggle, and the telly was all weird (Portuguese Bart Simpson, anyone?), and my mp3 player died because I didn't bring the right plug thing, and after Fishvom Day

I was a bit scared to eat all the stinky little dishes of Peculiar that they wanted to get so I just ate lots of chips. OMG lardiness. Though yay for a country where they think superfrazzled doughnuts and hot chocolate goo is breakfast.

Less yay for pervy blokes everywhere going "Pretty, English, love you" the minute you walk out of the hotel, though. Even if a bit of me is all "omg attention, I do not ming after all!" which obvs is Wrong and Bad and makes me a failure as a modern woman, throw me out of the sisterhood etc. Monster was obvs unimpressed at her now being officially too old/coupled to get sexually harassed, though, lolz. And Dad was Mr Possessive Freakout and threatened to beat people up, which he probably thought was Manly but made me want to curl up into a tiny miniature nothingperson till he stopped. Please to not be getting arrested, silly man. The police there have GUNS, dude.

Plus Dad and the Monster were all shouty and bitey with one another, which he said was just because they were on holiday and holidays are stressful. Er, wha? What is the point of holidays then?

| | |
|---|---|
| DAD AT HOME: | Today we are going to drink coffee until our tongues are black and gritty, then I will cook something with red peppers in even though I know you think red peppers make everything taste of marker pens. We shall spend the evening watching me read What Car? magazine and ignoring each other in front of the telly. |
| MONSTER: | Hooray! This will be the Best. Day. Ever. |
| DAD ON HOLIDAY: | Today we will get up insanely early for breakfast even though it is served until 10. Then we will march the frozen streets |

admiring buildings/paintings/gardens full of dead things that are supposed to be really nice in summer, stopping for coffee every half hour to thaw out ears, fingers, etc. In the evening I will drink beer and become annoying.

MONSTER: WTF, asshat? Shops are warm. This is supposed to be a holiday. I DON'T EVEN LIKE COFFEE. *STAB STAB*

Mmm, funola. I wonder if maybe they are like that always except when they play Pretendy Happy Family for when I am there. Urk.

Am now going to read all about the Dirty Midweek and observe other people's lives which are MORE FUN THAN MINE MOAN MOAN.

(Yes I know I just went on holiday and am a spoiled selfish tart. ;)

UPDATED:OMFG.OMGOMGOMGOMGOMGOMGOMGOMGO MGOMGOMGOMGOMG.

**HAPPINESS DEADLINE:** 60 days

COMMENTS

**frantastica**

Didn't know you were back today! Have been horrendously bored without you, sweetie. Sorry the holiday wasn't the best, but at least the hot chocolate was gloppy.

**serafina67**

Have you been to o jon o? GO THERE NOW.

**daisy13**

I'm sorry you didn't enjoy your holiday more.

Anything I can do to cheer you up?

**serafina67**

Umm. Not really right now. I just got some bad news.

**daisy13**

What kind of bad news? Are you OK?

**serafina67**

Sort of tricky to say cos I know who might be reading. But then the pix are online so it is not exactly a secret.

Umm. Think me and my bf just broke up.

**daisy13**

I am sorry. *hugs*

**serafina67**

Thx.

**daisy13**

What happened?

**serafina67**

He went away with some other people from school on holiday and someone put the pix online from the holiday. And ummm.

They are at o jon o. He is the one with the long hair.

**daisy13**

I can't see any pictures.

**serafina67**

NM, they're gone now.

**daisy13**

I'm really sorry. I think I can guess what happened without the pictures. No one should treat you like that. You deserve better.

**serafina67**

Aw thx.

**frantastica**

Whoa. Can I come over, honey? You're not answering your phone.

**serafina67**

Turned it off cos SOMEONE keeps trying to call.

Would love to see you but Mum wants to have dinner and hear about bloody Spain. And I am a mess anyway.

**frantastica**

Fair enough. Call me later if you want though, sweetie?

**patchworkboy**

PLEASE PLEASE PLEASE TURN ON YOUR PHONE?

---

7.56 p.m. Thursday 22 February | **i love my mummy**

Dinner = bunnies!

Not actual bunnies, obvs. But sausages and mash where you make the mash a big blob of a face in the middle and then two sausages are ears and one is a smiley mouth and tomato sauce for eyes and peas round the outside for grass/nutritional value.

*is five*

She is a nutjob but she is hella cute sometimes. Was having rubbish miserable day, and she came home early from work specially and we did weeping and hugs and the traditional All Men Are Bastards convo. Apparently the first boy who ever dumped her did it by getting his best mate to tell her best mate, only the best mates got it mixed up and she didn't get the message and she turned up at the "disco" (lolz) all tarted up thinking they were still going out and she just thought he was acting really weird and in the end he just yelled "I DUMPED YOU, GO AWAY" at her in front of everyone. Zomg. She was going all pink in the face just remembering it. She showed me some photos of her when she was sixteenish and she is all tiny and wee and big-eyed, like a little Bambi-person. I wish I looked like her. Minus the Gigantic Hair, blue mascara etc obvs.

Plus frantastica sent me comedy spam and made me giggle. Girlz Rule.

P.S. to SOMEONE: Srsly knock off with the phone thing because I am not going to answer. And don't bother commenting because I will not read it.

**HAPPINESS DEADLINE:** 59 days

COMMENTS

**patchworkboy**
PLEASE let me explain?

**frantastica**
Call me anytime, sweetie, ok? And check your email. *hugs*

**o jon o**
OK, honestly it is not as bad as it looks, I swear. And I know you won't believe it from him but you can believe it from me.

**frantastica**
Oh yes, the impartial best mate: so much more likely not to be a liar.
Just leave her alone, all right?

**daisy13**
That's really sweet. I thought you weren't getting on very well with your mum at the moment?

### serafina67

She is lovely really, mostly it is me that is useless and screws it all up. She has a crap job with a crap boss which makes her get growly over nothing at all and I get growly back and then we end up sitting in separate rooms or we will just go on growling louder and louder. But then she does dorky stuff like bunnies as a sort of love-you-really sort of thing, or I make her a cup of tea and curl up on the sofa with my head on her knee. We are like cross little stopwatches who get crosser and crosser till one of us presses the reset button and puts us back to zero. We are not very good at proper conversations, though, because she is always knackered and I am, um, evil. And she has been disappearing off to talk to Della lots lately about IDK what so tonight was extra-lovely. We went through the rest of her photos and giggled at Grandma's minidresses and floofy hair and Icklemum in orange dungarees, lolz.

### daisy13

Sounds like you two are very alike.

What about your dad?

### serafina67

Alike, eek! Scary idea. My mum is quite flaily and unconfident and headinthesandy and omg you are right, I can blame her for everything now! *headdesk*

My dad is the same, I suppose. Not flaily etc, just the not-good-at-conversations bit. Only I don't see him all the time, so we don't ever have the time to reset our stopwatches. I don't know. I am trying to be all positive and yayful about his wedding etc because not being is sort of unhelpful to everyone. But we don't ever do proper parent-things like argue about whether I've done my homework or just sitting about yawning. It is all trips to funfairs and Yes Of Course You Can which is sort of the opposite of what everyone else's dad is like. Except every now and then when he suddenly gets all deranged and tries to ruin my life for totally random reasons until Mum or the Monster or someone tells him to stop. So it is hard to know, really.

Oops. Am being v boring. Sorry, am in thinky mode now apparently.

**daisy13**

Don't apologize!! I like hearing what you think.

**serafina67**

LOL, you shouldn't say that cos I will emosplurge at you daily.

I like talking to you, though. It's nice to have someone older than me and sort of different to talk to. I sort of like explain things to myself when I explain them to you.

**daisy13**

Who says I'm older?

**serafina67**

IDK, you just seem like you are. Not in a bad way or anything! georgia_darkly is, like, at uni, and I don't even know about 8utterflywings. It's no big. ULife is supposed to be all about meeting new people.

Soz, didn't mean to say wrong thing. *flails*

**daisy13**

That's OK!! I am a bit older than you. I'm really glad that doesn't bother you.

**serafina67**

*hugs on lovely daisy*

**11.04 p.m. Thursday 22 February** | **some thoughts**

Partly gakked from an email convo from frantastica because she is way cleverer than ickle old me and made me think sensible things:

If people decide to do something, then they have to deal with what happens afterwards. If you eat eleventy bars of chocolate a day you will be fat. If you go with some h0r from Year 13 then your girlfriend will stop being your girlfriend. These are quite simple rules, really. Life is quite simple, really.

Being drunk does not make it OK.

Putting it on the internet "to prove it was only us messing about" does not make it OK – especially when your mate then takes it down cos he realizes he's dropped you in the poo.

Nothing at all makes it OK.

OK?

**HAPPINESS DEADLINE:** 59 days

---

**1.10 p.m. Friday 23 February** | **recipe for happiness**

As devised by frantastica:
  dvds with Johnny Depp in them
  mini jaffa cakes
  peanut m&ms
  ~~bombay mix~~ (WHAT is that smell?)
  duvets

Method:

Put all on sofa and mix till cheerful.

This is so perfect someone should make a montage of us doing it with cheesy pop soundtrack and me tearing up old boyfriend photos. Except they are on my phone so that might be difficult. Still I am doing one of those things like sleepovers in posh pyjamas that girly girls do in films etc like I am a real person. Woo. It is like a valuable life experience ~~and not miserable at all or in any way failing at making me forget I am lonely and woeful and probably dumped because of eating too many peanut m&ms already.~~

*slaps self*

frantastica has pointed out that I am the LAMEOORZ for typing when there is JOHNNY DEPP AS A PIRATE right in front of me.

Arrrrrrrrrrrrrrrrrr!

**HAPPINESS DEADLINE: 58 days**

---

3.29 p.m. Saturday 24 February | **Crazy Pete is Actually Crazy Shock!!!**

Don't even know where to start.

Not mentioning the whole thing where SOMEONE turns up on the doorstep in the middle of the night (well practically) and hammers on the door and SINGS and totally scares the crap out of me and Mum and then won't go away. Errr no that is not going to make me forgive you? And you should maybe never do that again. And if you were going to do it again you should probably not be drunk.

Mum says I should be flattered, and told me some horrendo story about some bikers she was dating fighting over her in the street and Grandad having to call the police. WTF? BIKERS? And since when is having people hitting each other over you supposed to be good? Way to be empowering single-mother-type-woman there.

And anyway, no one is actually fighting over me. I just got dumped by picspam, which is not really the same thing. :(

Apparently it is not the sort of thing you should mention to Crazy Pete either. I told him about the whole breakup thing and he totally missed the point and started going on about the DANGERS OF THE INTERNETZ OMG. And how people think they can be more honest when it is online because no one can see you but that is actually a big fat lie. And I said that he told me to keep an effing journal duh and he was all wakjfijriwfjwsok?

Apparently the point of a journal is for it to be something private and personal, where you can say the things in your head which you can't say anywhere else and that you hope no one else ever knows about. And so me putting anything here where other people can read it is me probably lying loads and pretending things about myself. According to Crazy Pete, anyway.

I dunno. I suppose I put things on here because they are the things in my head, and the things in my head may explode into another Incident if I don't let them out, so it is sort of necessary to have a place to put them. I am Eeyore and the internet is my useful pot to put things in, k? And if people like to read what is here then that is cool, and if not they can go away. It is better than talking to him, who can't tell me to go away because he is being PAID to listen to me. It's not like I tell him every single thing that is going on. I see him every other weekend and will have forgotten half of it anyway.

And anyway I wanted to talk about the whole weirdness of Mum and her Suddenly Going Out Lots, and how Dad has turned into Mr

Overprotective Father Who Wants To Phone Me Up And Do Talking, and how I am really angry with myself because he has moved a kajillion miles away to the New House that I don't even know what it looks like, and I will see him like maybe twice before the wedding, which makes me sort of not want to see him at all because ABANDONMENT OMG. Except I don't even know why I am upset about it because I don't even want to see him, only RESOLUTIONS OMG. And how the HAPPINESS DEADLINE is starting to freak me out because it is just reminding me that there have already been, um, THREE HUNDRED AND EIGHT DAYS already since the Incident for me to fix my life and become HAPPY in and I have not managed it yet. And how it is my birthday next week and I am going to be 16 and omg just like LIFECOASTER oh please let me get off and have a little sit-down and a think without having to do anything else for just a little bit?

And Crazy Pete wanted to talk about hair dye. Mkthanx.

I suppose if it was a "proper" diary I would have written those things down here maybe. But OH LOOK I JUST DID. :P

And I suppose there are things I would put here if SOMEONE wasn't listening. I would not be typing out song lyrics and then deleting them. I would not have to pretend to be all unteary and unbothered to prove I am not broken into little bits. I would admit how much time I have spent looking in the mirror and thinking about lolbabe and about chocolate and how confused I am. And OH LOOK I JUST DID IT AGAIN.

And maybe I should not have said that on here. But if I just wrote it down in a notebook and put it under the bed what is the point?

Ack. My brain hurts. Going to wallow somewhere in emo fashion. Want to listen to suitably doomy music and all my moping CDs are from him.

**HAPPINESS DEADLINE:** 57 days

**daisy13**

Crazy Pete doesn't sound very helpful!!

I hope you don't stop writing things here. I would miss you if you stopped.

**serafina67**

I will keep writing. It's sort of in my brain now, I think. Wherever I go I'm always thinking, "Ooh must remember to put that in later". When I was in with Crazy Pete I was just thinking omg must write about this and not really paying attention at all. I even make up sentences while I'm walking home from school, really impressive-sounding ones with jokes in. Haha, you can tell it was half-term this week. *facepalm*

It's like I was trying to say the other day, about needing to talk to people who are different from just your friends. I mean, my friends are lovely and spesh and sometimes it is sort of reassuring to have people around who have known you for ages, and know about the Incident, and are maybe a bit more forgiving then when I am useless, even if we never really talk about that stuff.

But then part of what's nice about ULife is the bits where I am not that girl. I am not in my horrid body or hearing my whiny voice or wishing I could hide the bad bits. And you don't know that girl anyway so you don't have me down as "that loopy one" or "the dumpy one" or "the one who hangs out with X and Y and Z so must like A and B and C". You just know serafina67, so I don't have to keep pretending to be someone else.

No idea if that made sense. Keep saying wrong things at the mo apparently.

### daisy13

Makes plenty of sense!! Maybe sometimes it's easier to put things here where it seems private, so you can say the things you wouldn't be able to say face to face.

Sometimes I think we can be closer to people online than the people we see all the time.

### serafina67

Ooh, get you! All profound and everything.

### frantastica

We're always here to listen, sweetie.

### serafina67

I know! Which is what Crazy Pete doesn't get because he lives in Old Man Cave Time and does not understand the internets.

*hits him with rock*

### cameraobscurer

*squishes*

Counselling types are totally ignorable. Screw im.

### serafina67

OK, that put the wrong pictures in my head …

(You are still talking to me? Is that ok?)

### cameraobscurer

Not going to ditch you just because Patch acted like a turd. Tore him a new one for you already. He is way sorry, if that means anything. I don't think they … you know?

### serafina67

Yeah, he has said sorry. A lot. But then my dad said sorry a lot to my mum and now he is marrying HER. The details are not really the important thing, you know? Think I am just unforgiving about some things.

Ta for tearing on my behalf, though. :) I suck at that stuff.

---

4.26 p.m. Monday 26 February | **humf**

Bloody Crazy Pete has made me feel weird about putting anything on here now. I was sitting in English thinking tum-ti-tum must remember to put in here that Simone Brasher said "LOL" and half the room went, "wtf does that mean?" and half the room went, "omg you twonk you don't SAY it." It was like a bonding moment in heartwarming American family drama where everyone's mum is amazingly thin despite spending all day at home baking muffins etc. And then a bunch of people sort of outed themselves with their ULifes and their MySpaces and their AIM names and then there was a bunch of other people all going "lala not telling" even though they had them too. And Miss K was all, "Ooh you are all writers woo! Only you cannot spell omg." And I thought, we could all be sitting here mostly hating each other all day and going home and talking quite happily online and never knowing. Which either makes us retarded, or brilliant.

Only now I'm thinking, wtf? Why did I need to write that down? Is it clever or lolarious or of great significance to the wider world at large? Will I need to remember it when I am old and lumpy and have sprogged out? Am I just doing it because of my oh-so-emo need for attention to boost my wobbly old self-esteem? No one out there cares what happened in French today, not even the people who were actually in French. But then Peter was all, "This should be about you, clotheaded sera who does not even get the basics of what a diary is, duh." So it should be up to me what goes in here, not him anyway. Except that was not really about me anyway.

DO. NOT. UNDERSTAND.

I only logged in because I am supposed to be writing a letter to my imaginary French penpal (penpal? Hello? Do they not have email in France or something?) and I really quite massively don't want to. Meh.

**HAPPINESS DEADLINE:** 55 days

COMMENTS

**cameraobscurer**

Ahh, the inevitable angsty "Why are we here anyway?" post. It is a blogger's rite of passage to one day look at their blog and think, er, why have I spent hours of my life posting bad photomanips of David Hasselhoff and YouTube links and awful sixth-form poetry instead of doing all the wonderful fun things the Kidz are supposed to do.

Congratulations. I look forward to the one where you change your layout entirely to black with tiny grey text that no one can read, closely followed by the one where you grandly announce that you are changing your username to l33t35k1m0 as an indication of your newfound maturity.

**serafina67**

You mean I am just predictable and boring and not all shiny-new with my fabulous profound life-changing thoughts? :P

Poetry? ;)

Who is David Hasselhoff?

**cameraobscurer**

Emo haikus. Yes, I am an asshat.

*Who is David Hasselhoff?*

Travesty! What are they teaching the young people these days? <u>Observe his manly chest</u>. ;)

**serafina67**

MY EYES, MY EYES!

That is some serious hair. But I am a bit worried about what he is doing to that car …

**frantastica**

Ma cherie, les Francaises ont "le email", bien-sur. Mais a notre ecole, ils n'ont pas les textbooks de more recent than 1982.

**serafina67**

Zut alors!

---

5.10 p.m. Wednesday 28 February | **sixteen**

So, birthday then. Woo. Yay. Balloons etc. *is Eeyore again*

Sorry, feel a bit plap about the whole thing. I liked it when you got taken to one of those ball pools and the whole class always got invited and people gave you selection boxes and toys and such. Now it's just a day where you go to school and about two people remember, and then you come home and celebrate with Exciting Homework and Telly cos it is a school night.

Also OMG 16 is like old and grown-up and people leave home and have proper jobs and lives with rent in them and having to decide whether they can afford shoes or cheese this week when they are THE AGE THAT I HAVE JUST BECOME. I keep looking in the mirror waiting to see a person who will be able to do all that. Um. Where are youuuu?

I am a dramahor, pls to be ignoring me and reading my Birthday Meme Rubbish what I am stealing off of 8utterflywings who did it the other week.

*Birthday Resolutions: on your birthday, list one thing for every year of your life that you would like to achieve, change, do differently, in the coming year.*

(Um, so obvs I have Resolutions already so I am cheating a bit, k? But they are only up until April 22nd anyway so... I have no idea how that is supposed to work. Moar rules pls?)

1) Carry on with the Completely Totally Honest thing, EXCEPT if it is going to make people miserable and, like, ruin their lives. :(

2) ~~Make new friends~~. Avoid messing up the ones I already have.

3) Continue to avoid Incidents, oh please yes.

4) Cheer up Mum. (Need to do better with this?)

5) Be more OK about wedding, Monster etc. (DEFINITELY need to do better with this.)

6) Talk to Dad. (Er ... yeah. *headdesks*)

7) OMG really for true shift spare tyre that is overflowing over top of my tights.

8) ~~Get boyfriend~~. ~~Get over boyfriend~~. Get a kitten. Kittens > Boys.

9) I AM NOT TELLING YOU THIS ONE BUT I KNOW WHAT IT IS.

10) Pass GCSEs non-craply enough to get into Year 12.

11) Shoes! The amazing ribbony black ones in Faith.

12) Learn to walk in the amazing ribbony shoes.
13) Convert entire wardrobe into things which go with ribbony shoes.
14) Discover fountain of money behind wardrobe to make these happen.
15) Be less massively shallow than this makes me sound?
16) ACHIEVE HAPPINESS DEADLINE. Then just put feet up for rest of year. :)

Imagine being 26 and having to have 10 more things you actually wanted. Though when I am 26 I will a) have a job and thus money to actually buy things and b) be too busy doing the job to spend all day on the internets doing stupid memes.

Anyway, apparently I am doing RUBBISHLY at my proper Resolutions.

I AM GOING TO TRY HARDER. STARTING TOMORROW.

Ack, have now missed Neighbours because I spent ages deleting things about shoes and then putting them back in again. :(

**HAPPINESS DEADLINE:** 53 days

COMMENTS

**frantastica**

Sorry you're feeling mis, hon! Come to mine at the weekend for a mini-party?

**serafina67**

NONONOoooooooooo! You were all lovely and sweet and fab and gave me beautiful things! Am just being daft and whiny. Plus some people remembered and left presents on doorstep that I DIDN'T WANT which is making me feel a bit grr.

Am going to some outlet place between here and Dad's new house on Sat to look for wedding-y clothes. Many many hours with Monster for company, erk. Would rather be with you. :(

**frantastica**

Poop. That doesn't sound very much like birthday fun.

**serafina67**

That's ok, Mum decided homework and telly was a bit pants as birthday fun too, so we are going to get a Chinese and watch stuff with pirates in again.

**frantastica**

Do you have cake? I have always thought cake was fundamental to birthday fun.

**serafina67**

In about ten minutes I will have spring rolls. I could stick candles in them? Except obviously not as they will not exactly help with the overflowiness.

**frantastica**

*bakes virtual cake*

**serafina67**

*eats virtual calories*

**cameraobscurer**

Jelly and ice cream?

**serafina67**

Mmm, boiled-up bits of dead horse! With frozen fat droplets suspended in water and sugar!

**cameraobscurer**

*barfs*

**8utterflywings**

16, woohoo! Aren't there things you can do now that you weren't supposed to do before?

**serafina67**

LOL yeah if you are worried about all laws and stuff. But I have no one to do them with anyway.

Soz for going off on one at that guy on your page. And for meme-stealing.

**8utterflywings**

Smackdown so totally deserved. Although remind me never to tick you off?

It's not stealing. It's sharing the love. :)

**adapted i**

Happy birthday!

**serafina67**

Thank you, whoever you are!

**georgia darkly**

Ponies > kittens.

**serafina67**

Ponies = less likely to purr/be purchased by Mother?

**georgia darkly**

You could put a bell round its neck and hope she didn't notice?

HB, btw.

**serafina67**

TY!

**patchworkboy**

Happy birthday xx

**daisy13**

Happy birthday!! Sorry you aren't having the best time. Didn't you get any nice presents to cheer you up?

**serafina67**

Make-up and make-up bag, perfume, digital camera, fishnet tights (omg my auntie is mental – and thinks I am a size "small", yay!), new trackies, CDs, vouchers, notebooky things. And probably some other stuff. So yes, am being totally ungrateful cow who needs a slap.

**daisy13**

Impressive list!! What did you like best?

**serafina67**

Prolly the notebooks and pens and stuff because frantastica made these collage things to go on the covers with all stuff I like so they are just for me.

**daisy13**

That's really sweet. I thought you'd say the digital camera. Didn't you say you'd wanted one for ages?

**serafina67**

Omg, you really do pay too much attention to my pathetic dribbly whining. It is nice, I suppose. I think Dad just got it so he can keep tabs on how lardy I look, though. I hate having my picture taken anyway, blech.

See: ungrateful cow. I am like Gadget Girl with all the stuffs I have in here. Slap me, for I am witch!sera who is spoilt and a bit disgusting.

ENOUGH! I am going to be POSITIVE and SENSIBLE and HARD-WORKING and by the Happiness Deadline I will be shiny-new and perfect. You totally have permission to yell at me if I am not these things, k?

**daisy13**

OK!!

OMG FEMALENESS IS HORRIBLE.

Did you read about that girl from Southney who got pregnant but thought she was just fat because she had eaten lots of crisps and had a baby upstairs while her parents were downstairs and then just went down to watch Coronation Street with them afterwards and left it in the wardrobe? And it was dead and no one knows if it would've been dead if she had not put it in the wardrobe and gone to watch telly?

Sex = bad.

Crisps = worse.

And now she is probably going to prison. Er, hello?

**HAPPINESS DEADLINE:** 51 days

COMMENTS

**georgia darkly**

Can you actually eat that many crisps?

**cameraobscurer**

THAT IS HOW YOU GET PREGNANT, OMFG!

**georgia darkly**

I see. Does it matter which flavor?

**cameraobscurer**

Yes.

**georgia darkly**

Crinkle-cut?

**cameraobscurer**

= wrinkly babies.

**georgia darkly**

This is way more educational than biology class.

**serafina67**

This is why I need to go on a diet! I CANNOT HAVE A PRINGLEBABY!

**cameraobscurer**

IT WOULD LOOK LIKE THE LITTLE MAN WITH THE MOUSTACHE AND THE BOW TIE!

**serafina67**

AAAAAAAAAAAAAAAAAAARGH!

**cameraobscurer**

AND IT WOULD SMELL OF SOUR CREAM AND CHIVE!

**serafina67**

*hides it in wardrobe*

**cameraobscurer**

OMG U R BABYKILLER!

**serafina67**

*guilts*

**daisy13**

It's really sad that she didn't have anyone she could talk to. I hope you don't feel like that?

**serafina67**

Xactly. And hello where were the parents? Yay for being a pathetic teenage singleton who does not have to worry about these things.

**daisy13**

Don't you have a new boyfriend now, though?

**serafina67**

New BF? Uh, no. Am still busy avoiding the last one.

**daisy13**

Not you and cameraobscurer? ;) Or should I not say that on here?

**serafina67**

Hee! No, cameraobscurer is a) a mate and b) not a boy. :D
Ahh, the crazy world of the Intarwebs ...

**daisy13**

!! Sorry!

**cameraobscurer**

Cameraobscurer would like to add that she wouldn't dislike
the arrangement at all, but sadly serafina67 only likes boy
parts. :(

**serafina67**

*blushes*

Way to make me sound like a h0r.

*is flattered, darling*

**cameraobscurer**

*plots your conversion*

**serafina67**

I think most of the people on here are girls. We are more
obsesso and navel-gazy, maybe. But the whole confusion
thing happens all the time, cos some people make stuff up,
and cos people don't want to give out too much personal
info obvs.

No one knows who anyone is really on the Intarwebs. Like
you WHO I STILL KNOW HARDLY ANYTHING ABOUT,
BETCH! You could be, um, Kylie or something.

Are you Kylie?

**daisy13**

No, I am not Kylie. ;)

**serafina67**

*is shocked* ;)

**10.45 p.m. Saturday 3 March** | **girls just wanna have ~~fun shoes~~ a bit of a sit-down**

Active pursuit of Happiness Deadline = TIRING. Zzzzzzzzzzzzz. BUT I win at travelling. Got on the train all by my lonesome (well, once Mum had put me on the right platform) and did the changes and got off in the right place so the Monster could pick me up, and then got on right train home again without aid of Dad who does not understand that trains are HARD and timetables are like just little lists of terrifying numbers OF DOOM designed to scare you and make you convinced you are on the wrong train and you will suddenly hear an announcement saying you are on your way to Norway or something. I know probably he is right and trains are not scary, but I've never actually done that before and it seems like the kind of thing I'd get wrong and I don't want to go to Norway. (There is a sea in the way, maybe? This is how much I don't understand geography. I am one of those statistical Young People that old people tut about who cannot point at Iran on a map. I am very very sorry.)

On the train I started a new VTN, which is about a girl called Cassie Peasgood (ordinary hair, ordinary eyes) who is at her father's wedding (erm SHUSH) when there is a big explosion and she is the only survivor. (No really SHUSH.) But somehow when everyone died their thoughts went inside her, so she has the memories of everyone who died at the wedding, and so she has to do all the things that the people who died wanted to do, like climbing mountains and posting letters they never wrote and that sort of thing. Word count: I don't know because I didn't take my laptop with me so it is all handwritten. But LOADS because omg, really long time on train.

Anyway, I have shopped till I dropped. And then someone

kicked me and made me shop some more. Shopping is supposed to be one of those things girls like, isn't it? Except that is obvs a clunky great lie made up by TYRANT GIRLS who

a)  like looking at themselves in mirrors
b)  do not have giant lumpy hips that stick out (see point a) and
c)  are not in the company of Monster on prowl for bridesmaid-who-is-daughter-of-the-groom-type Frock From Hell/Zara.

There was much grappling with my ferocious locks and attempts to demonstrate up-do which resulting in me looking like a hairy pineapple. There was a short ~~argument~~ discussion about whether I like people staring around the curtain while I am in just my knickers and pulling it back so an entire shop and even some passers-by outside can see. (FYI: I do not like it. FYI to people who design changing rooms: what is so wrong with doors? Do people have a front curtain on their house? No they do not. Grow clue please.) There was also discussion of us having matching outfits, followed by her going, "Maybe people will think we are sisters!" and me going, "Er...?" and her realizing that perhaps that is a bit on the Unspeakably Wrong side. *facepalm*

To be fair (*coughs*) to her I am probably not the helpfullest of bridesmaids, because when she says "What do YOU like?" I go, "Converse and jeans" and even my fashion-retarded brain knows that is probably going to look a bit mentalist in the photos. And it was nice of her to ask my opinion even if my opinion was "I don't know nuffin, find me dress help help?" And she bought me sushi and a giganormous mochaccino even though it meant we had to go to two different places for lunch. And she lied and said things looked nice which didn't to make me feel less miserable. In fact basically she was supercharming and fabu and I was grumpy and a cow. WOULD YOU LOOK AT THE FAIRNESS OF ME? I am so nearly almost liking her.

She is Good at Shops, too, which made me realize that I am Bad at Shops and I didn't even know that was a thing you could be bad at. Like, if there is no shopladyperson there for me to go "?" at in the changing rooms then I just stand there for a bit feeling ridonkulous and hoping someone else comes along and fixes it by asking first. And if they don't then I run away and don't try things on at all. But Monster goes "hello hello" and finds shopladypeople and no one minds. Where do you learn this? Is there a bit of school everyone else is going to that is, like, useful, where they teach you train timetables and how mortgages work? Because all I'm getting is chromatography and Siegfried Sassoon. Unless my adulthood is going to involve unexpected amounts of poetic emo about felt pens, I am borked.

Anyway, have dress. It is green, which apparently "accentuates my eyes". This is politespeak for "distracts from your arse", yes? Also have shoes, which I will have to practise walking in so I look less like a five-year-old playing in Mummy's wardrobe.

Actual Mummy thinks I will look spesh, though, yay. She wants me to do a miniature fashion show tomorrow (was too knackered when I crawled in from train) after she pointed out she will not actually see me in this thing otherwise. This seems mean and evil to me, but then I suppose if she was invited that would be a bit madcakes. This is why not to get divorced, children: the guest list is uber-complicated.

And Dad gave me some cash to shut me up when I went a bit sniffly at the station, which I felt a bit bad about because OMG expensive dress from shop I would never have even looked in and then shoes as well, and he just took me on holiday, and birthday present, oh noes. But there were flowers in the shop when I was waiting so I bought some for Mum because probably dropping me off to go and try on bridesmaid's dresses was not very nice for her, and she has been all nice to me and not said anything, even when she is maybe a bit blarg about all of that, and I was feeling a bit blarg myself about doing better at the Happy About Wedding Resolution than the Making Mum Less Glum Resolution. So now she is all smiley and chuffed, even though I had to explain that they were from me not from Dad because her face went all weird, and then she was all, "You should not spend your money on me," so I was all, "Never mind Dad gave me money," which was a thing, and way to totally ruin a present, self. *clonks self on head* But she liked them really. And now I feel better cos I spent his money on a nice thing, not on me. She has put them on the kitchen in the middle of the table in a big vase and now the flat smells like, um, flowers. Don't know what kind. Yellow ones that smell nice. *fails at knowing about flowers as well as Norway*

OMG, that was longer than any of my coursework. Going to bed now. Zzzzzzzzzzzzzzzzzz.

**HAPPINESS DEADLINE:** 50 days

COMMENTS

### frantastica

Forgot you were going away today, hon – sorry for email spam!

I hate going on trains on my own. I have to do it for concerts, and I live in fear of being told off for having the wrong ticket, or not being able to get the door open, or someone stealing my violin off the luggage rack. Horrible.

**serafina67**

I know! Why do they have doors where there are no handles and you have to dangle out of the window of a speeding train to open them? And the timetables are all just zomg NUMBERS OF NO SENSE and then weird men get on at the same time as you and you just know they will come and sit next to you just to freak you out even if you put your coat and bag and sixteen magazines all in a pile on the seat.

*hugs*, btw. Sorry things are so crappy at home. Emospam me any time, k? And I will actually reply and not be on a train ~~to Norway~~.

---

11.23 a.m. Sunday 4 March | *flumps*

Arg. Have just tried on dress to show Mum. Don't know if it was different lighting in shop or if Monster put E in my mochaccino but yesterday I looked OK and today I look like a Man In Drag. A short man. With a big bum. ~~And way too much boobage on display~~.

And it is not just me being barking because Mum got that look on her face when I came downstairs that basically says "Oh My God how completely hideous only I can't say that let me smile now *cough ahem* Yes Dear very nice". Now I know where I got my crapulousness at lying from, anyway.

Dress is now hanging on bedroom door glaring at me. Wedding is looming like a big looming thing. Carp carp carp.

2.29 p.m. Sunday 4 March | **Obesity epidemic omg!**

Dress Trauma made me take everything out of the wardrobe and try it on and WOW I hate all my clothes. And the body that tries to squeeze itself inside them. And I possibly might not be able to do up my only non-horrible jeans, cry cry woe.

Then I went and had lunch, and Mum had done pizza to cheer me up and that made me cry cry woe for real, all over the pizza. (Wet cheese = ew.) And I ended up telling her about the Happiness Deadline (with edited bits obvs) and she sort of looked at me wonkily and cried too, which, um, sort of isn't Making Mum Happy.

BUT she was all wooful about being "proactive" like Crazy Pete and so I actually *quivers* weighed myself. And I am not, like, American-sized. Mum says hormones and maybe still growing (nuh-uh, woman, I am a shortarse and you are stuck with me) and all of that make it more likely to go up and down. And I have recently suffered a tragic break-up. But still, y'know, I am quite lumpy.

So: plan! Me and Mum are going to be girl-like together and have a Healthy Eating Plan and go to the sports centre thing to jump up and down. We nearly were going to go to Weight Watchers but we both chickened out because it sounds scary (and also because Mum is not actually very lardy at all and is only really doing it for me, awwwbless). Plus she thinks I am made emo by not having enough vitamin B-something and doesn't want me to be all obsesso-diety. We are going to be obsesso-fitnessy instead as that is more ~~socially acceptable~~ healthy.

There are 40 days exactly till the wedding, which is totally enough time for me to be more perfect-looking by then. (Have realized main wedding problem is more this than the Monster these days. *is outstandingly self-obsessed*)

Maybe I will lose so much weight the Evil Drag Queen Green Dress won't fit any more and I will have to buy a new non-hidjus one. MOTIV8!

Or more likely I will just have to wear it anyway, and everyone will go, "Ooh, used to be a fatarse, then?" and the whole thing will have been a total waste of effort/celery.

Want chocolate now.

*fails at thinness*

**HAPPINESS DEADLINE:** 49 days

COMMENTS

### frantastica

You could come to circuits with me and my mum? It is super-early in the morning so before school, work etc. I don't always go but I'm sure Mum would take you anyway, if that wasn't too peculiar.

### serafina67

Aw, thx. Mum wants to go to the place by her office, not the gym thing by you, though. If I don't go with her she will just stay at bloody work instead and I will end up eating Coco Pops out of the box or something, which is sadly not part of the new Healthy Eating Plan. Plus if I go with her she pays. :)

I would say come too but I think Mum quite likes it being just us.

**frantastica**

That's sweet. Mine only takes me with her to prove there is something she can do better than me, I think.

**serafina67**

Mine is being all dorky and cute at the minute. I think she has the guilts because she is never here and I have become Tragically Neglected.

**georgia darkly**

American-sized? :-P

**serafina67**

Behold my ability to insult whole continents!

**georgia darkly**

Truly I am so insulted I must eat this whole box of Nilla Wafers!

**serafina67**

Truly I do not know what Nilla Wafers are but I wish to steal them from you!

**daisy13**

I bet you already look beautiful. But maybe getting fitter would make you feel better about yourself. You should keep a record here so we can all see how you're doing!!

It's good that you're getting on better with your mum now, even if she's busy a lot. Is she home from work late every night?

**serafina67**

Yay for my ULife Cheer Squad! And yes, think being a bit less of a lazy arse will make me less rubbish all over, hopefully. Exercise is supposed to make you have more energy or something. Never noticed this in PE but then most of that is spent trying to avoid showing your knickers to the neighbourhood in a stupid teensy netball skirt. Do the boys have to play rugby in their pants? I think not. IT IS OPRESHUN!

Mum might as well go to work in her PJs and just sleep under her desk at the moment. You are a PA, woman. Mr Boss Man is not going to die because some filing doesn't get done, ffs.

**daisy13**

That must be lonely for you. :(

**serafina67**

Not really. Della (who is the lady who lives in the flat upstairs) comes down to check on me sometimes. (Will have to remember to tell her not to bring cake, grr.)

I quite like being on my own, though. And anyway even when she is in, I am on here talking to you guys half the time. You are never alone with the internet. :D

*hugs blogfriends*

**daisy13**

*hugs you back*

---

5.49 p.m. Monday 5 March | **skience is wrong**

School = vom. Or skience is, anyway. Why can three people who are all sitting on one bench for the rest of the lesson not carry on sitting on the same bench to do a stupid experiment thing with watching some water boil? Why is watching some water boil something that can only be done by two people? (Why do we need to watch water boil is obvs the real question, because OMG kettles? I can make myself a cup of tea without need for Mr Davies and his is-it-hair-is-it-a-wig? mystery head.)

Hum. I am just bitter, because it is always me that says "OK, I will move then" even if it means I have to be in a pair with B. Who smells. And is creepy. And is BAD AT WATCHING WATER BOIL. Srsly, all she had to do was turn on the stopclock and write down some numbers. Davies goes, "Ooh a class graph on the white board" and everyone read out their times and when he got to us she was like, "11:46" and we were all, "Ng?" and it turned out that was THE TIME.

Maybe this is why she smells. She has a tragic fear of water and could not bring herself to press the button in case some steam hit her and made her a bit clean. Or she is a superhero who deflects all wateriness. (Worst superpower ever! Unless you are drowning, obvs.) Although actually her uniform is skanky in a falling-apart way as well as a dirty-stinky way, so maybe they are just poor and can't afford to have a washing machine and I am a satanically nasty betch for even mentioning it. Bad sera. :(

Still, I am definitely not going to put down any of the skiences for my "I would like to do THIS please because I am very very interested in it and also clever, no really" AS Level thingies. So it doesn't matter.

Mother, where are youuuuuuuuuuuu? *is hungry for nutritious salad items*

**HAPPINESS DEADLINE:** 48 days

## COMMENTS

### frantastica

I promise I'll move next time? Sorry, I thought you didn't mind.

B has a brother who's really ill, I think. We were in primary together and they used to wheel him out at sports day. That sounds really terrible. Oh dear.

You are still going to do French with me? I don't know anyone else in that class at all!

### serafina67

OMG, I remember now. He has ... erm ... muscular dystrophy? Cerebral palsy? What is the one with all the coughing? Arg, am probably being totally offensive. Even while I'm trying to be all sympathetic and non-evil. Gah.

I don't know if I'll get the grades for French. And anyway Mum is now going "Ooh, do sociology" just because she went to that parents' thing and thought Mr Turlyebekova had a shmexy voice. *eyeroll*

### frantastica

I will be sympathetic about the brother and the smelliness. But having an ill brother isn't an excuse for her being a complete cow.

She was not very nice to me in primary.

### serafina67

*squishes little primary frantastica*

### cameraobscurer

All superpowers are win. Don't be afraid, tiny child! Neverneedinganumbrellagirl to the rescue!

### serafina67

But what if the tiny child has fallen down a well?

**cameraobscurer**

Neverneedinganumbrellagirl will call in her sidekick, Occasionallyneedsanumbrellabuthasreallylongarmsboy? And they say the superhero genre is dead. Fools!

**serafina67**

*commences new VTN AT ONCE*

**cameraobscurer**

And it is a wig. Totally. Real hair cannot be put on backwards when you are unexpectedly woken up on a school trip. FACT.

**serafina67**

*sporfles*

---

09.20 p.m. Wednesday 7 March | **I am a cat/dog/plank/warrior/thing that hurts that has no name**

Me and Mum went to Active Yogalates, which was very 90s Madonna of us, but sounded less like it might make us die than Aerobic Blast and Ultimate Body Condition 2. Seriously, why not just call it Don't Come To This One, Lazy Unfit Person?

There was weird thumpy/relaxy music and lots of lying on your back like a lost woodlouse (if lost woodlice were also attempting to create some stomach muscles to do stomach muscle exercises with). Some of it was dead easy and made me feel all bendy because there were even fit-looking people there who couldn't do some bits. And then some of it was involving of Teh Pain and the possibility of pukiness. And then there were some totally wtfish bits where you stand on one leg and ~~wobble until you fall over~~ gracefully extend arms and legs until you are an aeroplane, and I have no idea how that's supposed to be good for you but it was quite funny.

There is a ginormous mirror all along one side of the room, so you end up catching little bits of yourself waving your legs in the air and looking stupid, which is not very helpful. But everyone else looks just as retarded, so it's not too blah. And Mum was all together and organized and chatty with the lady who does it, in that Capable Grown-Up way that I envy liek whoa. Sometimes she is as uselesslike as me and runs away and hides from things where you have to talk to strangers etc, but tonight she was all Normal. Probs this means she is quite happy at the moment, maybe? Woo. We did chatting in the car on the way home, and she has total mentionitis about this Ray bloke from the next-door office. Mummy has a crush, lolz. She went all pink when I told her not to misbehave. Although that might just have been the Active Yogalates.

**HAPPINESS DEADLINE:** 46 days

COMMENTS

**cameraobscurer**
*pheers you*
**serafina67**
*fears ginormous mirror more*
**daisy13**
Well done!!
**serafina67**
Go me! I am all aching and broken now too, so it must have

been good for me. And I have eaten nothing but vegetables and the occasional slice of ham all week so far. (This is Not Actually True, but, you know, effortless! Woo!)

**daisy13**

You should feel really proud of yourself. *hugs*

---

5.02 p.m. Friday 9 March | **the internets is where we are honest and true**

Which is apparently something I said at Cam's and is now a phrase. I am quotable, people! I am taking over the internets and claiming them as my betch! Y'ALL DO MY BIDDING, HORS!

MEEEEEEEEEME. Gakked from cameraobscurer, and she was all ouch-ingly honest in hers so now I have to be.

*Write a list of what is under your bed. Tell the truth, no matter how embarrassing. Do not run to the bookshelf and throw in some Tolstoy to make yourself look intellectual.*

Oh noes, cos my bookshelf is just groaning with Tolstoy. ;)

OK, I could cheat, because I have drawers under my bed, so under them is probably just some fluff and maybe a spider. But I will behave. So, in the drawers is:

- two big woolly jumpers that are too woolly to go in my chest of drawers
- some tights which have holes in the toes (why am I keeping these?)
- sandals
- some books from when I was at primary school (aww so cute!)

- a photo album of pictures of me looking like a little barrel (including the one where I am dressed up as a flowerpot – no I don't know why – which is the one and only picture of me I don't hate)
- letters from Dad
- UGLY SHOES OMG
- some certificates for swimming from when I was about 12
- a recorder
- some music for the recorder (I CANNOT PLAY THE RECORDER WHY IS THAT HERE?)
- some notebooks with some old bits of diary in
- some notebooks with VTNs in them
- compilation CD with the Joints on *spits*
- an old mobile phone
- an empty fag packet with a lighter in it
- my old mp3 player
- some batteries which I think are dead but am not quite sure enough to bin them in case they aren't
- an empty Smirnoff Ice bottle wrapped up in a scarf which I don't think is even mine (the scarf, not the bottle, that is mine, oops)
- a book with OMG rude sex parts in it
- a pencil case
- a woodlouse
- ~~my emergency chocolate~~ the wrapper from my emergency chocolate

From this (unbelievably long) list I draw the following conclusions:

- I have learned how to do bullet points on this thingy. WIN!

- I really should start throwing things away
- I am horribly embarrassed by my own existence. Seriously, I had to go back through and put them all in a different order so all the really embarrassing ones weren't all in the same place. And now I quite want to deletedeletedelete, because I feel all jumpy. But sort of pleased because truthful, yay!
- You should never read old diaries. Because the 13-year-old you? Humiliatingly lame. (Unlike this me, who is, er, also lame. But less lame than that one. Oh please let it be true?)

**HAPPINESS DEADLINE:** 44 days

COMMENTS

**cameraobscurer**
Is the scarf black with silvery threads going through it? Because I lost one of those.

**serafina67**
It's a woolly one. Sort of fluffy and pink. And you have never been to my house.

**cameraobscurer**
Probably not mine then. ;)
Where are you, btw?

**serafina67**
Lolz, sorry. Have to eat yucky diet stir-fry thing and convince Mum I am still allowed out. See you there?

**georgia darkly**
I have a recorder under my bed too. Bizarre.

**serafina67**
Maybe your recorder and my recorder should get together

and make beautiful music together. Apart from them being recorders which can only make nasty squeaking noises.

**frantastica**

Under everyone else's bed is more interesting than mine. :(

**serafina67**

That is because your mum is a Neo-Nazi with a Dyson and will have removed all Things of Interest. It is no reflection on you.

**frantastica**

It is no reflection on me that my mum is a Neo-Nazi?

**serafina67**

*facepalm*

Someone take this keyboard away from me plz?

**daisy13**

I'm trying to work out which ones you think are the embarrassing ones. ;)

**serafina67**

Urk, try all of them!

---

11.37 a.m. Saturday 10 March | **significant post of personal musings etc**

Decided I had better put something on here that was Proper Diary-type stuff, not just omglieksquee! rubbish as usual, since I am going to see Crazy Pete in a few hours. He will probably yell at me anyway and still tell me I'm doing everything wrong, but at least this will rescue me from feeble attempts at lying, which OMG I am appalling at apparently. Was supposed to be in at 11 last night and at 11 was actually lying under a bench down the beach while cameraobscurer made helpful suggestions about how to conceal Perfume de Bacardi by pouring Coke all over my favourite silver top. Thank you darling. Thought my "lost my mobile and then found it again" excuse was pretty damn spectacular at the time but Mother has been making Bang Crash Slam noises with cupboards all morning, so think she may suspect I have a hangover. Which I don't, weirdly. Though I do have a very sticky silver top that is apparently only supposed to be dry-cleaned. (Dry-cleaning is the crazy, no? You give people your clothes and they steal them for a bit and when the clothes come back they are supposed to have been cleaned. Dryly. It is all an OBVIOUS LIE and all they have done is spray lots of Febreze around hopefully. Which is what I am going to do. Take that, Sketchleys!)

Um. That was not very Proper Diaryish. The trouble is there are lots of Proper Diary-type things to say, but they are all a bit ouch-y. And obvs there is the Complete Total Honesty thing, but then there is the omg I know who might read it SHUSH NOW thing. Which is annoying because it is exactly what Pete said last time about the Dangers of the Inturnuts. *sulks*

I know Proper Diaries are for yourself, not to be some conversation or Fern and Phil phone-in or whatever, but that is only because of them being from Ancient Times and there not being the technology, right? If Anne Frank could've blogged instead of writing things in a little notebook, she would have. It would've been less rubbish and miserable if she'd had other people to go "Oh noes, you live in a bookshelf, sympathy pat on head." If it was now, there would be a whole online community of dispossessed Jewish people sharing ways to put carpet on the bottom of their shoes so as not to be noisy, and 101 Recipes for Mouldy Bread, and all of that.

Erm, I am not comparing myself to Anne Frank there, OK? Or saying "Lalala, she would've had a lovely time if only she had had a laptop," cos, duh. I am just wibbling and talking metabollox so I can keep putting off the thing I sat down to write about, which is ...

Um.

Arg.

Mum is totally seeing that Ray bloke from work.

See, I have written it down now so it must be true.

And now it seems sort of small and unimportant compared with, like, Nazis. And actually it is totally small and unimportant even not compared with Nazis. Wow, I am just SO VERY OFFENSIVE TO EVERYONE OMG.

Cos in a wonky way, I am totally happy for her, because she is a bit more skippy and cheery than normal, and that is probably better than her coming home and sitting on the sofa in her trackie bottoms watching telly (even though that is a totally acceptable way to spend a Saturday night, k?). And I am totally getting a freebie on the Resolutions there what with her turning into Goofy Cheerful Mummy without me even having to do anything.

But then there is a bit of me that is a bit sulky. Like, I only know about it because Della came round to ask for her shoes back (yes, my mum borrows other people's shoes, ew gross etc) and she was asking Mum about last night and I went to get some rice cakes and heard them. WTF, Maternal? She would go crazy batcakes if I had a sekrit boyf. What am I going to do, ground her?

And then there is the whole "me not having a sekrit boyf" or any other kind of boyf either. Or a kitten.

And OK, yes, I am probably sulky as well because OMG, I have one

147

dad and he is useless enough already. YES I KNOW IT IS NOT ALL ABOUT ME REALLY AND I AM BEING PATHETIC AND IMMATURE. And I know I am getting a teeny bit ahead of myself there cos hello, they are probably just ~~shagging~~ temporarily holding hands and it will all be over tomorrow or something. But then that would make Mum all gloomy again anyway which would be horrible/Resolution-killing.

LOOK! IT IS ALL ABOUT ME AGAIN!

Off for shrinkage to talk about ME some more. More whining later, probs.

UPDATED: Crazy Pete is an asshat.

**HAPPINESS DEADLINE:** 43 days

COMMENTS

**frantastica**
Maybe you misheard them, sweetie?
**cameraobscurer**
*puts all parents in washing machine*
*turns on spin cycle*
*watches*
He still goes on about you all the time, you know. Just in case the kitten thing doesn't work out …
**daisy13**
Sometimes people keep secrets for good reasons.
What did Pete say?
**serafina67**
Pete was urk-making and weird and made me cry, like,

loads. I can't believe my parents pay a man to make me cry.

**daisy13**

Poor you. *hugs you tight*

**serafina67**

*hugs back* Thank you, need hugginess. :(

---

5.10 p.m. Saturday 10 March | **Zzzzzzzzzz**

OK, being this emo is exhausting. I am kerknackerated and I haven't even done anything except sitting and the occasional snotpowered whimper.

Pete was his usual Crazy Pete self and made me feel about two feet tall. Waaaah. Apparently the reason I am weirded out by the idea of Mum getting porny with Invisible Ray Who May Not Even Exist is because I am afraid this means I am being replaced. Er, dude, I am her daughter? And he is (possibly, depending on invisibility/existingness) her bloke? Not. The. Same. *headdesk*

It is making me a bit bonkers, though. Help?

*You are in a dark, damp cellar. On the left is a trap door, marked "ASK YOUR MUM ABOUT HER SEX LIFE". To the right is a fraying rope ladder, labelled "RUN AWAY, PRETENDING YOUR MUM DOESN'T HAVE A SEX LIFE". Which do you choose?*

**HAPPINESS DEADLINE:** 43 days

149

## COMMENTS

**georgia darkly**

Run away. Fast.

**serafina67**

*You climb the rope ladder. The fraying ropes crumble under your hands, and you plummet to a splatty death.*

**georgia darkly**

Splatty death is still better than asking your mom about her bits.

**serafina67**

Bits? OMG.

**cameraobscurer**

Word. You don't want to go there. Start poking about in her business and she will want to poke back.

**serafina67**

I have no business! I am footloose and business-free! My MUM can pull and I can't. BRING ON THE SPLATTY DEATH!

**cameraobscurer**

Dude, you could pull in a heartbeat.

**serafina67**

That would not be pulling. That would be "giving in because you keep going on about it".

**cameraobscurer**

Who, me? :P

**serafina67**

No, him. :P

**cameraobscurer**

And you would still be reading his ULife because ...?

**serafina67**

Um. It is crammed with helpful maths revision tips?

**frantastica**

Trap door. Otherwise you'll feel awkward, and she'll guess
you know anyway?

**serafina67**

*You open the trap door, and jump. After a 100-metre drop,
you land on giant spikes which pierce through your brain
and kill you instantly.*

**frantastica**

Owie. Maybe not, then.

---

11.32 a.m. Sunday 11 March | **Zomg**

| | |
|---|---|
| MUM: | Good morning sera! Have some freshly-squeezed orange juice and some kiwi fruit. Whee! |
| OUR HEROINE: | Um. What? It is Sunday. Zzz. |

*twangly noise*

| | |
|---|---|
| MUM: | Aha! A text message. *smirks* Now, my beloved and only child, tell me about school. And boys. |
| OUR HEROINE: | Are you on crack? |
| MUM: | Boys are nice, aren't they? |

*twangly noise*

| | |
|---|---|
| | *more smirks* |
| OUR HEROINE: | Is there something you would like to share, Mother? |

MUM:          *turns pink* *is a nine-year-old*
OUR HEROINE:  *eyerolls fondly*

Well, that solves that, anyway.

She says it is "complicated" and it is "not a relationship" and might come to nothing. I say: awwwww. She is so entirely doing that cute thing where you start liking someone and you feel all fluttery and confused and everyone else can tell and you think you are the only one who knows. Their office must be weeing themselves watching all this.

Big wet raspberries to Crazy Pete, anyway. BEHOLD MY MATURE RESPONSE TO MY MUM ~~AND HER BITS~~!

**HAPPINESS DEADLINE:** 42 days

COMMENTS

### daisy13

It's nice that she's so happy. Are you really OK with it? You seemed upset before.

### serafina67

I think I was bummed that she didn't tell me before I sort of found out by accident. But then I can sort of understand why she might not want to be all "Ooh, new boyf" if it is new and babysteps-ish.

Anyway, she is happy! So I can tick her off my Resolutions. At the moment, anyway.

### daisy13

I can think of lots of reasons why she might have kept it quiet.

I bet there are lots of things she doesn't know about you.

We all keep secrets sometimes.

**serafina67**

But that is MY life! I am supposed to have secrets, I am a teenager. She is a grown-up woman with a car, she is supposed to be a bit past naughty snogs round the back of McDonald's.

Mmm, hypocrisy. :)

**frantastica**

Your mum is adorable.

**serafina67**

LOL, I know. She cut my kiwi fruit up into little chunks for me and everything.

---

7.59 p.m. Monday 12 March | **because you lot are cleverer than me**

And I am too stoopid to work this out for myself.

serafina67 is:

[ ] impressively win and feministical in her sternness about Unforgivable Boy

[ ] pathetic and alone for no reason

[ ] STILL going on about this, wtf?

(You can pick all three if you like. That is what I would do.)

**HAPPINESS DEADLINE:** 41 days

## COMMENTS

**frantastica**

None of the above? (You did not include "justifiably being a touch hesitant, yet undoubtedly will make correct decision" as an option.)

**serafina67**

*points and larfs*

**frantastica**

*hugs*

I'm possibly not the ideal person to offer advice here, alas.

**serafina67**

*squishes*

**cameraobscurer**

What about "SO going to snog him again anyway at some point so might as well get it over with and sod all this 'forgiving him' bollards"?

**serafina67**

Um. IDK.

**cameraobscurer**

"Giving up on Boys altogether, Unforgivable or otherwise"?

**serafina67**

LOL.

**georgia darkly**

I guess it's a trust thing, right? Whether you trust him not to cheat. And I don't know the specifics, and I don't know the guy himself except from him being kinda dorky on here, so … *shrugs*

Alone =/= pathetic, btw.

**serafina67**

Alone = feels kind of pathetic when it is not necessarily, um, necessary.

And yeah, is trust thing, but it is sort of complicated. Like how if I trust him again it says more about me as a person than it does about him, kind of? And the whole Happiness Deadline thing is to do with me being kind of Happier About Who Is Me, not just, you know, happy. So I need to not stuff up.

---

Dear The Government,

GCSE coursework = the suck.

How about I just write you a little note to say I promise I know things, and then we can forget all about the Giant Maths Project of WTFness I have to hand in on Friday. Because, really, is it going to help anyone to have to look at some diagrams that I have ~~downloaded from the internets~~ carefully crafted with my own special hands? It is not.

Yours,

sera xx

Arg. Careers Day is in like two weeks and we have to do the straw poll thing where you put down options for next year and I am TRYING really honestly but omg now every single thing I do wrong is like IMPORTANT AND LIFE-RUINING. And that is before we even get to the last exams, which I have to be all Calm about.

*stares at happiness deadline*

*tattoos it on brain*

*crosses fingers*

COMMENTS

### cameraobscurer

I would chuck you mine but last year's was probably different. 2D sequencing involving bread products. Mmm, mathematical doughnuts.

### serafina67

No fair! You get doughnuts, we get "Designing a Garden for Wheelchair Users". Who apparently have wheelchairs which are one square of graph paper wide. Handy, that.

### frantastica

You forgot to mention that the wheelchair users have a fetish for not putting pink paving stones next to yellow ones (except at corners). And the silly garden designer has ordered twice as many pink paving stones as yellow! Gosh!

### cameraobscurer

I am now thinking about fetishistic wheelchair users. Visuals are … unusual.

I liked when maths was sums.

### serafina67

I liked when maths was not DUE IN ON FRIDAY OMG.

### frantastica

It's only 10%. You'll be fine. Can't email mine because it's in pencil on graph paper (you read the thing about no computers, right?), but I'll show you tomorrow.

### serafina67

No computer? Argh.

I know! School's gone old-skool.

---

**9.11 p.m. Thursday 15 March | Urg**

lolbabe was in my Active Yogalates class.

*flails*

I was totally looking forward to it, and feeling all positive and self-helpful because I have been good this week about eating cucumber and brown rice and ~~pink wafer biscuits two at a time~~ fishes. And then I walked in and saw her and we both kind of went GAAAAAAAAAAAAAAAAAAH and hid. Sort of. It is hard to hide in a room where there is a huge mirror all along one side. Apparently it is a good thing I do not want to be a spy as it turns out I would be rubbish at the "pretending to fiddle with your shoe" thing while hoping people do not notice you are there.

I think she was going to come over and say something, maybe. But then Mum saw her too and just kind of put me on the other side of her, like she was a sort of cushion. And then at the end I thought maybe I should go and say something, but then I just kept thinking about how I looked all red in my face and my hair was all sweaty and I was in some old trackie bottoms that make my arse all baggy, and she was all so so perfect-looking and beautiful like always, and I felt like I would just be this pollutant in her air.

And OMG I know she got perfect-looking from starving herself etc and I should feel like I'm better off because I will not have my bones fall apart when I get old or grow fur on my face and all of that, but at the end of the day she is still thin and I am still wobbly.

I wish I had an eating disorder. It would take all the stress out of dieting if I had some disease making me fear the sight of a KitKat Chunky.

And yes, the bit of my brain that is, you know, *brainy* knows I am talking BOLLARDS. Please to not hit me, kthnx.

Anyway I had a bit of a sad cry in the car on the way home, and Mum threw her handbag at me while driving because it has tissues in, and it hit me on the head, which made us fake-argue and LOL and feel a bit less rubbish. And then we sat in the kitchen and did talking and had herbal tea, which tastes ~~of feet~~ delicious.

Mum says if she still has an eating disorder then probably she looks in the big mirror and sees a fat person anyway. So she could be eating any old crap really, and it would make no difference. But Mum says she looks a little bigger and healthier, and she wouldn't be able to do gym classes and stuff if she wasn't eating, so maybe the centre where she goes now is all helpful and working. I hope so.

It's weird, because I feel like I have to say "No, really, I DO hope so" like it won't be real or believed, and probably no one else even cares anyway because they don't like her. But Pete says you should listen out for times when you need to explain your feelings to other people, and ask yourself why you are doing it. He calls it "protesting too much", like you only say it because you really really want it to be true, even if it isn't. And maybe I do want her to be better now just so she can come up to me and say "Thank you, sera! What you did was the best thing that ever happened to me and now I am magically cured thanks to YOU oh yay forgivenesses!" If I was in a movie then that is what would happen. But things don't get cured and mended and tidied up like that. I am not all cured and mended and tidied up either.

Is weird seeing her though. We were like BFF, and now, poof.

*huggles friends* Don't go anywhere, nice ppl!

**HAPPINESS DEADLINE:** 38 days

## COMMENTS

**daisy13**

BFF?

**serafina67**

Best Friends Forever.

Apparently without the Forever part, obvs. :(

**daisy13**

Ah!! I understand now. It's nice of you to want her to be well now, after everything that happened.

**serafina67**

Not really. It was other people that gave me all the hassle and did my PE kit and all of that, and they were just trying to be good friends and be all supportive of her. Which probably makes them less horrible people than me who was, um, not.

**daisy13**

You're very generous!!

Maybe you could be friends with her again now?

**serafina67**

I am a different person now, I think. Hopefully, anyway.

**frantastica**

Not going anywhere, sweetie!

**serafina67**

*clings*

**frantastica**

BTW, my mum says yoga will only burn 192 calories per hour. So you might want to do something like spinning instead?

**serafina67**

OMG, srsly? *cries*

**georgia darkly**

Still here, chickadee.

Any progress on the Unforgivable Boy decision?

**serafina67**

Urk. Not really. But there is a party thing down the beach tomorrow and he will prolly be there. And he has been reading all this so maybe we will have to do Talking or something.

**georgia darkly**

ULife: bizarrest dating agency ever.

---

11.49 p.m. Friday 16 March | **inevitable boooze blog**

Am drunk.

Am online.

Badbadbad. Ooops. Goig n be in troubleLIEK WHOA!!

**HAPPINESS DEADLINE:** 37 days

**10.43 a.m. Saturday 17 March** | **Sorry**

SORRY
SORRY
SORRY
SORRY
SORRY
SORRY
SORRY
SORRY
SORRY
SORRY

That is more to cameraobscurer and everyone who left messages on my phone than to patchworkboy. But it is to him too.

I am an awful person and I deserve to end up dead in a ditch or something.

**HAPPINESS DEADLINE:** 36 days

---

**12.02 p.m. Saturday 17 March** | **Stop! HAIKUTIME.**

Haiku meme, because I feel too awful for actual posting and I don't deserve more than 17 syllables.

*All comments must be in haiku form.*

I got drunkified
I did things I shouldn't have
I am a bad girl

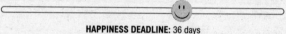

**HAPPINESS DEADLINE:** 36 days

COMMENTS

**cameraobscurer**
No one is angry
Just be careful with yourself?
For we adore you

**serafina67**
Someone is angry
I promise never again
Feel like death now *voms*

**cameraobscurer**
Cherry Lambrini
Is the root of all evil
And makes your tongue pink

**serafina67**
LOL it really does!
If only that could explain
What my pink tongue did :(

**georgia darkly**
I did not know that
LOL was just one syllable
Educational

**serafina67**
Educational

It is my middle name
And not Jayne at all
**georgia darkly**
My middle name is
Ermintrudycaroline
Handy for haikus
**frantastica**
You *are* a bad girl
Haikus are nature poems
Mention frogs next time
**serafina67**
Also there should be
Like philosophical things
As well as the frogs
**frantastica**
I would hug and more
If only I did not have
To leave room for frogs
**serafina67**
Counting syllables
Makes my brain come out of my
Ears. Argh. Stuff this. *hugs*

---

6.43 p.m. Saturday 17 March | **thinkage**

OK, after last night's asplosion of lameassery I'm all thinky today and feeling a bit spun out, so am going to produce a Post of Emoness. It was this or a VTN about a girl called DeadFace who has black hair and black eyes and a black heart and sits around all day shouting "DeadFace", word count: 903, all of which are "DeadFace", oh you get the idea.

The contents of my head, in no particular order:

I have post-booze panic and feel so crawlingly guilty I could die. I had about two hours of celebrating the end of the stupid Maths Project of Doom where I thought I was the fabulousest thing on the planet, and there was definitely some singing, and I was flirty and beautiful and witty and who would not love me? And then I saw Patch and got all confused and decided to unconfuse myself by drinking more. Erm. And then everything goes a bit spinny and peculiar in my head, because it seemed like all of a sudden Cam and everyone had gone somewhere else, and I was with all these blurry people at the pier, and Patch wasn't anywhere and then I sort of woke myself up and realized I was snogging a boy. And then I think I sort of carried on snogging him. And then I had to have a wee behind some rocks, and then I think I got all upset and I don't really know what it was about. And I was with the wrong people to be having a big emofit with and I was sick and oh arses.

And I sort of do know what it was about, because even being drunk I knew I was doing something awful and guilt-making, and that was sort of why I was doing it. Like witch!serafina had overheard princess!serafina's silly embarrassing imaginary plan involving hand-holding and campfires and moonlight, and decided to stamp on it tlll it broke. Like witch!serafina does with all my Resolutions.

And Mum's there this afternoon handing me tissues and saying I'm so lucky, I have such a lovely life, I have all these things that she never had and isn't it nice how I have good friends who care about me, and parties to go to, and this whole life ahead of me, and everything so uncomplicated, and she wishes she was me sometimes.

WTF? Are you blind, woman? Are there really actually two of me, and one of them is going off and having a stressless glorious time of it, being all independent and not having to go and sit in a classroom full of stupid people I hate for hour after hour? Sera II, who can watch TV whenever and eat what she likes and never has revision piling up like a bitch in the back of her head and lives with a mummy and a daddy who wuv her very much and never fight.

And now I'm whining over the parentals and the divorce again and THAT WAS TWO YEARS AGO AND NOTHING TO DO WITH ME DURRR. It isn't that. It is and it isn't.

I just feel like I'm losing. I feel all prickly in my own skin, like I'm trying to crawl out from inside it, only then when I do I want to crawl back in and hide under my hair. I want to stay in bed for ever. I want to not have to sit in school and be interested. I want to get out of there and do something less pointless with the rest of my life and I have no idea what that thing is. And everyone is all "Haha, you only need to get 17% in your final maths exam to get a C" which only makes it worse because then what sort of spoon would I have to be to stuff it up? I want to be able to decide when I get to eat dinner, and not have to grovel for lifts whenever I want to go anywhere (Mum's taxi service, ahahaha, yes, you are so very hilarious, HELLO I DO NOT HAVE A CAR AND I DID NOT CHOOSE TO LIVE TWENTY MINUTES BY BUS AWAY FROM THE REST OF HUMANITY). I want to not be in my stupid pink bedroom looking at the stupid balloony wallpaper on a Saturday night because I am grounded for being stupid and drunk. I want to be happy. I don't even want to be happy, I just want to be OK.

I don't know. I can't figure out if I am just being teenage and whiny and emo, or if I am actually going proper mental. Which is really scary. Like with The Incident, it was just like something went CLICK in my head and made me chuck a total fit and I didn't see it coming or anything, I just was really angry. When I threw that chair I just needed to DO something or I was going to explode. And I totally didn't mean for it to hit anyone, especially not Miss Stevens, who was actually about the only person by then who was still being nice to me and not just assuming I was a useless write-off they could shove at the back and ignore, and OMG I totally never meant for her to leave even though people said it was cos of other stuff and not just that, and I felt as bad about just that as I did about all the rest of it, and I even wrote her a card but I didn't know where to send it so I never did. But anyway it was completely this accidental thing like someone else had done it and then after I'd done it I didn't really know what to do so I just ran away and locked myself in the loos and hid there and wouldn't let anyone in for like hours and everyone thought I was nuts and smashing the place up but I only threw things about a bit one time so they would stop trying to come in. And really I was just sort of embarrassed and worried about being in trouble and there being loads of questions and how everyone would think I was mental (which, um, not really fixed by locking self in toilets). I was just trying to hide really. And then it turned into this big thing and suddenly Mum was outside in tears, in school, in front of everyone, and OMG totally couldn't come out then.

And it wasn't like it fixed anything. It is just this unbelievably embarrassing weird thing that happened that for a bit everyone wanted to TALK about in school and at home, and then they wanted to pretend it never happened, and I still want to do that. But I can't, because it is always there like a toothache, and no matter how nice or kind other people are and say "Oh I am sorry I hope you feel better toothache is horrible" they can go off and forget all about it, and you can't. So I am still here, wondering if someday I will go CLICKCLICKCLICK again, and being really quite frightened of that. So I need the Happiness Deadline to hurry up so I can prove I have not gone CLICKCLICKCLICK for a whole year. But I need to do things to make the Happiness Deadline actually be, you know, true, and I am just. so. tired. Not angry or asplodey or insane, just tired. And sad. Nothing complicated. They are like the little words you learn on flashcards when you're small because everyone feels them. This is just ordinary. This is just what life is like, maybe. But if this is what it's like I don't want it any more. I just want it all to go away.

God, I am such a farking sterotype. OH NOES OBSERVE MY EMO PAIN AS DEMONSTRATED BY MY HAIR DYE. Only, like, not. Usually I can sort of laugh at myself for being so pathetically obvious, and predictable, and teenage angstish, and right now all I can do is cry.

OK, now I feel worse. I am really sorry I was such a useless selfish thoughtless h0r yesterday and I will understand if you all hate me. Now going to go and watch Casualty and eat a million crisps. (Am leaving comments on but will probably not reply, just so you know.)

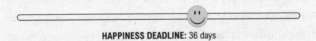

**HAPPINESS DEADLINE:** 36 days

COMMENTS

**cameraobscurer**

I want to say I know exactly how you feel, but I hate it when comments to this sort of post are all "let me talk about ME ME ME", because that's not exactly helpful. I think 1) you feel extra-crappy because of the hangover 2) wandering off and getting drunk with a random crowd and snogging a random bloke is not the most sensible thing in the world, which you know because you aren't thick (and because we all left you screamy messages), so you're maybe beating yourself up a bit about that and 3) I think you're right about the self-sabotage business, with Patch especially, but maybe you were trying to hurt him a bit as well as yourself. Not getting at you, baby, I promise.

I don't think you are "mental". But you might have depression or something like that. And you are already seeing Crazy Pete, and he should be able to help you with that if you are depressed.

Anyway, we love you whether you think you're mental or not. *hugs* (And next time we will take better care of you.)

### frantastica

*hugs tightly*

I don't say it very often but I feel like that all the time. Most days I get up and wish I could walk out of the house and never come back. Everyone thinks I have this perfect life where I get straight As and distinctions and we all sit down as a family every night to have a roast dinner and talk about how wonderfully middle-class we are. But I don't think anyone's life is really like that. My parents hate one another. Mike is squatting in some hole in London because he had a row with Dad, only no one is allowed to mention it. Cath is on anti-depressants because A levels are making her lose it, only we're not allowed to mention that either. So I'm supposed to be the "together" one who will uphold the family honour, so I can't drop piano or violin or dancing or they'll know I'm not. Those were things I started because they were fun, anyway, so I had fun things that weren't just school and studying and exams all the time. But they aren't fun any more. Nothing is fun any more.

If I could dissolve, could disappear completely, without it hurting anyone, I would do it right now.

### frantastica

Oh god, I just read what Cam put, and that is exactly what

I just did. I didn't mean to ignore you and only talk about me. That was really selfish and stupid of me. I'm really sorry you're feeling down, and probably knowing that everyone else is too won't make you feel any better. *loves you*

**daisy13**

I'm sorry you feel so sad. I wish I could give you a real hug!!

---

10.43 p.m. Sunday 18 March | **emoflail**

Oof. Was attempting lie-in and then got woken up by epic yelling from Mother on phone. "This is like being 14 again, tra-la-la," I thought, and also, "Oh FFS, she is breaking up with Ray and will be miserable again". Only it really was being like 14 again because it was DAD she was yelling with. *headdesks*

So then she comes in to go "Blah blah your father SIGH wants you to meet your future step-grandparents EYEROLL on the first weekend of the Easter holidays HUFF as well as you going down for the wedding on the 13th DOUBLE HUFF you don't want to do that do you HINTY EYEBROW" which would be fine (only not obvs) if I was not also being texted by Dad saying the same thing (without the actions as he is not that good at texting).

So looks like my holidays will be fantastic and so very holidayish. Which is probably a good thing as after Easter we have like 4 weeks in school before exaaaaaaaaaaaams OMG possibly I should do some work.

Not sure I deserve fun anyway. Still very sorry about Friday night and making people worried. Still wondering WTF I was thinking. I am a screw-up. Please don't hate me.

**HAPPINESS DEADLINE:** 35 days

COMMENTS

**frantastica**

No one hates you! *loves*

And you are not a screw-up.

**cameraobscurer**

What she said. :)

**serafina67**

But this is why I am hiding, because I have flailed with supermassive proper emo and now people feel like they have to say nice things back again in case I go mentalist and off myself or something.

THIS DOES NOT MEAN I AM GOING TO OFF MYSELF, K? I AM JUST SAYING IT AS AN EXAMPLE. I am not one of those mental attention-seekers who write about how they are cutting themselves or whatever and then sign in as a RL "friend" and say that they have committed suicide so they can read all the messages from random people about how lovely they were, and how everyone should have taken them more seriously.

It's like every single word I say needs some extra thing to explain what I meant. Is there an emoticon for "ignore all of this, I am just being crap for five minutes and will be fine really"?

**cameraobscurer**

~~>8:(~~ ?

**serafina67**

Wow. There actually is. :D

**daisy13**

Do people really do that? Scary!!

**serafina67**

The internet = more crazy than you could possibly imagine.

**daisy13**

I wish I could do something to cheer you up. I thought of you a lot yesterday.

**serafina67**

Aww, you are too sweet. I'm fine. Just boringly emo.

**daisy13**

Do you mean that or are you just trying to make other people feel better?

**serafina67**

~~>8:(~~

---

4.54 p.m. Wednesday 21 March | **i would like to be an astronaut/train driver/mechanic (pick one)**

Careers Day. Woo.

So basically it was lots of teachers going, "Blah my subject is the best and most fun and you will get to watch telly for it, whee, only OMG it is also verreh verreh hard work and you need to be the cleverestest and shoo, go away, only please do apply for it or I will look like a cack/unpopular teacher and the others will all mock me, only really you will need an A before you even think about it, eff off" etc. Which was, um, confusing.

And then there was a man with a beard to help us match up Our Future Career Plans What We Of Course Have to subjects. Because apparently if you want to be, like, a German translator, you should do German, yo. Who knew? Also he had to tell us how most of the jobs on his list didn't even exist in his young day (no, really?) and how very lucky we are.

Is this something that all teenagers get, this You Are Lucky thing? Or are we actually supposed to be extra-lucky? Cos if so, I do not want to travel back in time to teenagerness of the past (not even with that shaggable Doctor Who man). They were all urchins who licked matchsticks up off the floor until their noses melted from the phosphorus. (I learned something in History! WIN!) I think everyone thinks that because we have laptops we actually have all learning downloaded directly into our brains and no longer have to make any effort. Which is a Very Good Idea and someone should invent it. But until then, er, no.

Anyway, we did this computer thing where you fill in tickyboxes that ask questions like "Would you rather be inside or outdoors?", where the answer is obviously "It sort of depends on what I am doing, you twonk", except there isn't a tickybox for that. And you just know that the computer will think "A vote for outdoors? You would like to be a Forest Ranger!"

But I filled it in because a) I have no farking clue what I'd like to be When I Supposedly Grow Up and b) because Mr Kean made us. And a little bit of my brain thought it might actually go "ping!" and come up with the best job in the world, which has SERA WILL LOVE THIS written on it in shiny red letters, and then I could stop worrying about it because a computer had said it was OK to be that. Um.

So apparently my destiny, my future, the thing I am doing all this stupid coursework for is:

*drumroll*

Human Resources.

Which is apparently not offering up my limbs for medical experiments (good) or becoming a baby factory (good) but working in an office hiring and firing people (OMGwhat?).

Maybe I should have ticked the I WANNA BE A FOREST RANGER box.

**HAPPINESS DEADLINE:** 32 days

COMMENTS

**frantastica**

Count yourself lucky: I got Librarian. My destiny is to wear my hair in a bun and whisper a lot.

**serafina67**

Noel got Police Officer. I think maybe we should not trust the Computer of Career-Deciding Doom.

**frantastica**

Noel as in Noel who sells *ahem* at the bandstand? OK, I feel better now!

Sorry I didn't see you after: piano exam tomorrow. (Which is not at all a Librarian-type thing to be doing, OK?)

**rishyish**

I got Librarian too. We both foolishly ticked the "I have ever read a book" box.

**frantastica**

You will look very special with your hair in a bun.

**serafina67**

OMG, is the entire school on here?

**rishyish**

Yup. *waves* Have added you, hope that's OK.

**serafina67**

*adds back* Yay! Soz about your stuff with L. (Went to read your place, hope you don't mind.)

**rishyish**

You give my attention-whoring heart a gentle glowing feeling. This means yes.

**o jon o**

When we did them last year I got Music Producer. :P

Are you coming to the gig on Friday?

**serafina67**

Gig?

**o jon o**

We have a new guitarist. ;)

**serafina67**

Yeah, Cam told me. Um. Don't know. Think I have, um, other plans already.

**o jon o**

Will put you on the guest list anyway. El Jointez miss our biggest fan!

**serafina67**

Aw, thanx.

**daisy13**

I thought you would get something artistic or a bit quirky from that sort of quiz. Designer? Architect? Writer?

**serafina67**

I did too. Am bummed at being just office-y person like everyone else. Though probably I should be glad they didn't come up with Bag Lady.

No, rly. Newly Boyfriended Mums say, "Yes sera you can go to the gig, come back whenever you like. And here is a tenner for a taxi home/chips/lager/condoms/drugs wahey!" Ray is clearly a Good Thing. I shall go to Crazy Pete ~~tomorrow~~ today (oops) and tell him he can stick his Fear of Replacement up his Crazy Pete Nose.

What would be really really extra-good is if Daughters of Newly Boyfriended Mums had places to go to that didn't involve Dealing With Consequences Of Own Behaviour. Which I should totally have to deal with, because OMG I am the one in the wrong this time, and hello! I see the irony and feel its bitey teeth. And really I have sort of got off lightly by just being ignored and maybe whispered about a bit.

The thing is that it is sort of hard to explain how I feel without sounding really outstandingly carp even by epic sera standards. But I think I just sort of liked knowing he was there maybe more than anything? Like he was in my pocket and I knew he was sort of waiting for me to change my mind and now I have ruined that. And now I have ruined it properly by saying that here where he can see it but Complete Total Honesty etc. And maybe in some ways I feel kind of relieved, because it is sort of decided now, and I don't need to think about it any more.

Anyway, it is necessary for me to be relentlessly single. It is my job now to stay at home knitting, baking and tutting at the clock. *It's 1 a.m.: do you know where your mother is?*

Talk to me, ppl! I am thoughtful and full of chips.

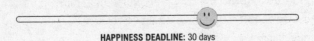

**HAPPINESS DEADLINE:** 30 days

## COMMENTS

**frantastica**

*waves from babysitting hell*

**serafina67**

Don't worry, you didn't miss much. Plus you are earning money and I am just spending it. Easter holidays fund = ninepence. :(

**frantastica**

No one has pooed up your sleeve today. I suspect this means you still win.

**serafina67**

*shudders* I would hug you but ew.

**cameraobscurer**

Didn't miss much? Worst review EVAR!

**serafina67**

OMG! I didn't mean it like that! The Joints were fabu as always and Tomtom was guitarry goodness and you were like GORGEOUS and that new one with the uppy-downy-slidey-bit (BEHOLD MY GRASP OF TECHNICAL KNOWLEDGE) was completely the best song you have ever done.

Sorry, was just a bit weirded by, you know, the obvious. :(

**cameraobscurer**

Best review EVAR! Except the new one with the glissando (behold MY grasp of technical knowledge, ha!) is a Beatles cover, you gonk. So best song we have ever done is prolly fair, to be honest.

You are forgiven. Mostly for calling me gorgeous.

Sorry about the boy, btw. He'll get over it.

**serafina67**

*fangirls you*

Re boy: that is sort of the problem, y/y?

**daisy13**

Sounds like you had a strange night!!

Maybe you should get a new boyfriend after all, to keep you company when your mum is out with hers. Or do they not go out that much?

**serafina67**

Nah, she is here most nights. She works in the same office as her bloke, so they see each other in the day mostly.

I am going to be a nun or something, I have just decided.

**daisy13**

!!

---

6.27 p.m. Saturday 24 March | **everyone's daughter should meet their mum's new boyfriend?**

OMG, am supposed to be in shower so I can go meet frantastica but must get this spoodge out of my head first or she will be stuck next to jiggly restless sera in the Vue and that would be a bit film-ruining, maybe.

So, Crazy Pete, blah blah blah. He says I am looking and sounding better, which means either his prescription needs renewing, or that chips and emo are good for me. Or that the Healthy Eating Plan, which we have sort of forgotten about, was totally working, and making me all shiny and perfect-like, and the recent chips and emo have just not kicked in yet. Erm. I did not cry, at least, which is quite win.

177

And he asked about the Deadline and made me feel a bit less hopeless about Resolutions by pointing out I have done some of them already, woo! Like, minor shrinkage has occurred, and Mum is wooful, and I am quite befriended. I am not sure the boyfriend one gets to be ticked off since it is not exactly a Thing For Making Sera Happy lately (and also I sort of mentally replaced it with Kitten) but if Crazy Pete Man says it counts then who am I to argue? So I have made progress and should Give Myself Credit.

Anyway anyway omg shut up and get to the point sera: Mum came to pick me up and was her typical current loony self, as in very skippy and deranged and let's go shopping and have cake in Puccini's. Woo! says me. Woo! says Mum. Woo! say Mum and Sera.

And who should happen to turn up in Puccini's moments later? Golly gosh wow, it's Ray! *sitcom audience applause*

Arg, am going to miss bus and have not changed and arg. Will tell you rest later, sorry, um, oops.

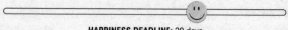

**HAPPINESS DEADLINE:** 29 days

COMMENTS

**rishyish**

You can't stop there! Cruelty!

**cameraobscurer**

*stays tuned for next thrilling instalment*

**cameraobscurer**

*taps foot* FFS, are you watching Titanic or something?

Sorry, sorry, distracted by romcom, lost bus tickets, bus tickets which get found again after you have bought a new one oh bumbumbum, sleeping, breakfast etc.

And now have built up suspense and it will be a letdown, because my mum constructing this whole ridiculous unveiling-of-bloke-in-café thing was the funny part, and the rest was mostly me going bright red and mumbling. Please to be giving me warning so I can construct Armoured Sera in future, Maternal Dearest?

Ray seems nice, in that "your mum has given me a list of Things To Ask Sera to demonstrate my non-scaringness" kind of way. So I have no idea what he is really like, because she didn't give me a list of Things To Ask Ray, and all I could think of was "Are you two at it then?" and "Does Dad know?" and similar Things I Should Not Ask Ray Under Any Circumstances Ever.

He is a bit older than her, I think (am rubbish at telling old-people ages). But he still has, like, lots of hair and is not all beer-bellied or anything. He has blue eyes and one of those scratchy red faces and he wore a stripy blue shirt and a dark blue jumper over the top and brown shoes, but in a these-are-my-expensive-casual-weekend-not-a-suit-clothes kind of way, not like from an Oxfam or anything. (Behold me making excuses because he was technically a bit minging and Mum is quite pretty and could do better, just in case he ends up related to me or whatever. Stranger things have happened.)

He made Mum go all giggly and poke him in the shoulder, though, which was quite cute. And one time, her hand was resting on the table, and he put his hand over hers, and she went pink and sort of slid hers out from under. She is all smitten but trying not to be in case I think it's weird, I think. Which it is, so score to her. Either that or she was just running away from his ManBling. Gold watch plus sparkly cufflinks plus gold ring? Lolz.

Oh well, at least Mum has someone to share her mid-life crisis with. Anyway, he bought me cake, so I have decided to like him for the time being. :D

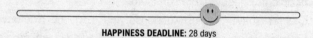

**HAPPINESS DEADLINE:** 28 days

COMMENTS

**cameraobscurer**
Sounds like it could have been much worse. You should see some of the trolls my mum has dragged through the front door.

**serafina67**
He was definitely some way above troll. But somewhere below ... um ... I have no idea what would be the perfect bloke for this situation.
SUPERMAN! I could use a step-superhero.

**cameraobscurer**
Perfect bloke? What is this myth of which you speak? :P

**rishyish**
Keep working that agenda, baby!

**cameraobscurer**
*polishes big gay hat*

**rishyish**
Cake is the way to your heart then?

**serafina67**
This is supposed to be news to anyone?

**frantastica**
You didn't tell me he wore ManBling! Or that he was old! We

definitely should've just gone for pizza.

**serafina67**

I know! That movie was zsjrh3iufhwaij. What is the point of
a romcom where they get together at the beginning?

**frantastica**

Exactly!

Sorry I had to whizz off afterwards. And for the bus thing.

**serafina67**

Is OK! Sorry I made you be late. Hope the parental rage
was not too scarifying.

---

5.02 p.m. Monday 26 March | **akwjr3 ui2nwfi**

GODBOTHERER HAVE SPLIT UP.

This is so strange. If that had happened three months ago I
would've been in tears. I would've been on the forum, sharing the
weepage with my fellow Botherers, refusing to play anything else
ever again, wearing my T-shirt in protest and very possibly writing
to my MP, whoever he/she/it is. And instead it took me till today to
actually notice even though the news came out yesterday (had
forgotten that email account, wow there is a lot of spam from
people who can't type in there), and I just feel sort of ...
unbothered.

Ahem.

I know liking them was some sort of dorky thing that I have
grown out of. I know they are sad and embarrassing and I might as
well have nailed a sign to my head saying "I am easily led by

marketing, sell me stuff!" because they were just some record company cashing in. I know I haven't listened to them in months and probably never will again. But I was a complete obsession whore for Jamie for a bit, to the point of imaginary marriage (it was a lovely day thank you, I wore red, he wore trainers, everyone said we were made for one another and we had a food fight with the wedding cake while GB played "Girl In The Wardrobe"), and sometimes I did actually think it might not be only imaginary. (OK, that's beyond embarrassing.) All my avatars were of him, and my MySpace was just pictures of him, and all the time I spend on here these days would have been all doing Botherer stuff. I even nearly went to his house one time with a bunch of other posters from the forum, just to stand outside and look at his front door, and the only reason I didn't go was because I thought if I ever met him I would say something ridiculous and never be able to look at his face again without remembering me saying something ridiculous and that would have ruined it.

Yes, I am that retarded.

But it was really really important to me once, and not even all that long ago. And it just seems to odd to have something go from being so huge and important to being hardly a thing at all.

And now I am laffing at myself cos I can just see me trying to explain this to Pete, and him going HELLO SERA SHALL WE DRAW SOME CONCLUSIONS FROM THIS? And me going UM I AM SHALLOW AND FICKLE AND I LET PEOPLE DOWN? (see Exhibits Kym, Patch, everyone ever). And him going DURRR NO IT MEANS PEOPLE CHANGE AND MOVE ON AND YOU ARE LESS EMOTIONALLY CRAPTASTIC NOW THAN YOU WERE EVEN IN LIKE JANUARY? And me going OHHHHHH.

*is going to have to start calling him Clever Pete*

**HAPPINESS DEADLINE:** 27 days

COMMENTS

**cameraobscurer**

I forgot you liked them. I think that was one of the reasons I used to think you were odd.

*does not have sekrit stash of S Club 7 CDs under her bed*

**serafina67**

OMG! Rock chick status ruinated 4eva!

**daisy13**

I remember growing out of things like that. Suddenly things which were really important stop being important at all. Don't feel guilty about it!!

**serafina67**

Thx. I can hardly be emo about it since Godbotherer = least emo band ever. And they are like 23 or something now and probably quite happy not making embarrassing pap any more. Yay me with the profound thinkiness though!

**daisy13**

Well done you!!

---

7.43 p.m. Wednesday 28 March │ **meme**

Gakked from rishyish:

*List six things you would like to say to six different people, online or in RL. Be as honest and direct as you like. (Do not say who they are!)*

1) I wish I was you.
2) F*CK OFF.
3) I love you loads and loads and I wish you liked yourself more. But sometimes I think you put it on a bit so people will tell you how much they care.
4) I miss you.
5) I don't miss you.
6) Sometimes I think we're really close, but I don't think I could ever say that to your face, which probably means we aren't.

Hmm. Not sure how #6 works if this is things I want to say to people. Oh well.

UPDATED: Hello, commenty people! It says I can't say who they are so I am not spoiling my Complete Total Honesty thingy. I am not telling! But omg you are a paranoid lot.

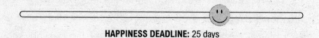

**HAPPINESS DEADLINE:** 25 days

COMMENTS

**cameraobscurer**

I bet I know who #5 is. ;)

**frantastica**

Am I one of those? Because if so, I'm really sorry. I really did mean to meet you to walk home but I had practice. And I know I've been really boring lately, and I'm really sorry.

**rishyish**

Please tell me I'm not #2?

**adapted i**

**adapted i**

This is the harshest one of these I have read. OMG!

**temper temper**

Friending you cause you kick ass, beeyotch (even if you did like Godbotherer once). (Here from cam's, btw.)

**serafina67**

I do? Yay.

**daisy13**

You're very direct!! Maybe it's a good thing we don't tell people the truth to their faces.

---

4.28 p.m. Friday 30 March | **season of plans/chocolate**

MISERABLE SCHOOLIE MODE DISENGAGED

EASTER HOLIDAYS MODE INITIALIZING …

COMMENCING CHOCOLATE-ANTICIPATION SQUEE IN

5

4

3

2

1

SQUEEEEEEEEEEEEEEEEEEEEEEEEEEEEEE! TWO WEEKS OF FREEEEEEEDOM!

OK, so actually it is more like two weeks of EEEEEEEEE EEEEEKDOM. Holidays look like this:

• Go to Dad's (on train on my own waaaah) to meet Monster's

parents/talk about weddingish things
- Come back (on train on my own whoaaa)
- DO EPIC MOUNTAIN OF HOMEWORKS
- Hang out with frantastica writing excellent VTNs
- See ~~Crazy~~ Clever Pete for injection of wedding-yay
- Eat chocolate eggs in very small moderate quantities due to wedding
- Go to wedding (on train on my own flaaaaargh)

And then I have like a week of school and then HAPPINESS DEADLINE.

icandoiticandoiticandoiticandoiticandoiticandoiticandoiticandoit
*crosses fingers*

**HAPPINESS DEADLINE:** 23 days

COMMENTS

**frantastica**

I can come over to yours if you want cheering? Dad has apparently been replaced by an android, and offered to drive me to somewhere I might actually want to go.

**serafina67**

Soz, would love you to but am booked: away all weekend so Mum says she wants to hang out. We are going to yoga thingy, then being sofabound and girlish. Sera > Ray, whee!

**frantastica**

That's OK. Have fun, honey. Call me when you get back? We can make VTNish plans …

**daisy13**

That sounds pretty busy!! Well done for going on the train on your own. Now you've done it once, the world's your oyster!!

**serafina67**

Yay! Am trying to feel all hardcore and non-wobbly about it. Mum just goes, "It's OK, if you get lost you can just ask someone for help" and I am like eekafiuewfj, since when is parental advice "Please talk to strangers"?

---

8.12 a.m. Saturday 31 March | **yawn**

OMG it is early. WHY DO YOU LIVE SO FAR AWAY, STUPID FATHER MAN?

Anyway, I am a) awake and b) weirdly overexcited about seeing ~~his~~ their new house even if it is far far away. Even though I have to go on a train on my own again and am a bit terrified.

So, predictions for my Weirdest Weekend Evar, puhleese: will Mr and Mrs Monster be

a) gummy and offer me Werther's Originals and want me to sit on their knee
b) evil and demand I am locked in a scullery/made to scrub fireplaces/sold to the white slave trade for magic beans
c) there is no c. Those are the only two options for step-grandparents.

The white-slave-trade option sounds OK. Would get me out of exams anyway. :P

You are all asleep, aren't you? Grr.

6.43 p.m. Sunday 1 April | **Fool fool fool**

ROLL TITLES

DIRECTOR: Hi. Welcome to the dvd commentary for Weekend at Dad's. It's a comedy, it's a tragedy, it's a crazy edge-of-your-seat runaway rollercoaster ride.

SERA: It really isn't.

DIRECTOR: The rollercoaster part was pushing it?

SERA: Unless it was an unfinished rollercoaster that lifted you high into the sky then plummeted you off a cliff to exploding death.

DIRECTOR: *scribbling noises*

SERA: ?

DIRECTOR: Just taking notes for the sequel. Oh look, here's where we introduce the guest cast. I think Marge Spoogelboogel does an outstanding job with the role of Mrs Monster here. There's a genuine air of menace the moment she appears.

SERA: That would be the perfume. Or the hair. Or the genuine air of menace.

DIRECTOR: And here's Mr Monster.

SERA: *yawns*

DIRECTOR: I think, looking back, perhaps the script here needed work.

SERA: You mean where he spent three hours talking about cars and then another one showing us his car and then he drove away?

DIRECTOR: I'm sure you learned a lot about cars.

SERA: His was red?

DIRECTOR: Erm. There was that moment where he pointed out that the wedding is taking place on Friday 13th? That was funny.

SERA: *snerks* I do not think the Monster thought so.

DIRECTOR: Yes, I think her expression there conveyed "fury" and "you are my parents so I can't stab you" quite beautifully. And of course, that wonderful crying scene after they left. Worthy of an Oscar. Or at least two tissues.

SERA: We seem to be skipping over the really embarrassing parts where I spilled red wine on the new cream carpet and broke the dishwasher.

DIRECTOR: I have edited them out to make you look more win.

SERA: Woo! I love you. Who are you again?

DIRECTOR: Um. Tricky. God, maybe?

SERA: I don't think I believe in you.

DIRECTOR: Meanie! I will make a director's cut and show everyone the bit where you had a massive row with your dad and told him you wished he was dead.

SERA: Bum. I knew atheism was a bad plan.

Well, that was a thrill.

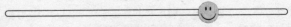

**HAPPINESS DEADLINE:** 21 days

## COMMENTS

**frantastica**

*hugs* Could have been worse?

**serafina67**

I could've broken the washing machine as well?

**daisy13**

I'm sorry things didn't go so well.

What happened with your dad? It sounds like you must have been really upset to say that.

**serafina67**

I totally win at trains. Go Team Sera!

The Dad thing was just me being Witchy and evil because I had managed to be lovely and Princessish for hours and apparently that was all too much. Gah. He gave me money instead of an Easter egg because obviously I have no particular need for chocolate. So I got all upset and shouty, and he got all upset and tried to be all huggy, and I got cross because I was still upset and you have to sort out the upset bit before you get to do the huggy "oh well never mind stupid emo child here's another twenty" part.

OK, that made no sense at all. I was being a brat and was just pissed off because I haven't seen him in for ever, and he doesn't seem to have even minded, really. So obvs when I do see him I act like a h0r to make sure he will never want me to visit again, duh. *is retarded*

**daisy13**

I bet he misses you really.

And I'm sure you're still beautiful, curves and all. *hugs*

**serafina67**

Awwwwww. *squishes*

Just back from Crazy Pete's. (The Clever thing was just a phase, apparently.) He was wearing a suit and a tie (with SNOOPY on it, WTF?), which apparently he always does in the week, and I only see him as JumperMan because I go on weekends. Which makes me think

a) he must always see kids on weekends, so does he wear the jumpers because he thinks it makes him look more friendly, or because he does not give a monkey's bottom what we young kiddies think?
and
b) I do sort of mind which of those it is.

It did seem quite weird, talking to this suity man. It was a bit more like being sent to the Headmaster ~~for telling Mrs Talbot to eff off in the middle of Business Studies~~ instead of talking to a fluffy waffly man who is annoying and nuts but still quite fluffy. Not that Mr F has ever worn a Snoopy tie, hee. Or asked me if my menstrual cycle has an impact on my mood, thank god.

Maybe I am just weird about clothes. I have tops that I wear to cheer myself up or sort of flump about in, and tops I wear when I'm feeling FABULOUS and which make me feel more fabulous, and a black sleeveless top thing that I only wear when I am feeling thin and a bit slutty, which makes me (possibly) look more thin and (definitely) act more slutty. (Have not worn this since January. Erm.) And then there are Fat Day trackie bottoms. And lucky pants. And, er, other pants. And now we are in a world of TMI and I'm shutting up now.

Do other people do that? Is it a girl-type thing? Or am I some kind of Speshul Clothing Freak?

Anyway, Suity Pete Man says I should not put too much pressure on myself with Resolutions and stuff, which I think means OMG SERA U R FAIL. But poo to him. I am so nearly there and I am not mucking it up now. *stamps foot in determined and non-bratulous way*

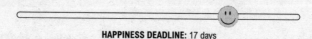

**HAPPINESS DEADLINE:** 17 days

COMMENTS

**frantastica**

It's not just you! I have a skirt that I would wear every single day if I could, just to cheer myself up.

**serafina67**

*feels less weird*

Does this mean Crazy Pete has to feel Jumperish every weekend? Or does the jumper MAKE him jumperish?

I am SO deep.

**cameraobscurer**

No pulling pants?

**serafina67**

Do the Lucky Pants not work for that?

*looks round for boyf*

Guess not.

**georgia darkly**

Sparkly red pumps with a bow on the front. Never fail to make me click my heels together.

**serafina67**

Sparkly feet = sparkly rest of you. *nods*

(Memo to self: stop wearing so much effing black, k?)

**georgia darkly**

But it goes so perfectly with the red shoes!

---

3.26 p.m. Sunday 8 April | **unhappy Easter to you all, tiny children**

Men? Complete and total twonkheads.

Mum has spent four thousand years today being all Nigella and turning the kitchen into the sort of disaster zone that may need the UN to come and pitch rescuing tents in it. She has made pastry, ffs. Who even knew that you could MAKE pastry? And proper roast chicken and roast potatoes and carrots and green beans (bleh) and actual gravy (note to self: never ever watch someone make proper gravy again) and then APPLE PIE with the pastry and mmmmmmmmm, the whole flat smells of win.

Except it did at about 1 o'clock, and then by half past it was smelling a bit burny, and then it started to smell a bit like stuff that was going cold and slimy so we ate it while Mum looked at the clock and continued to say, "He did say he might get held up, gosh he is so busy, it must be something v v important, poor him."

And then she burst into tears and I didn't even get any pie.

Ray = git. He has not even phoned. I quite liked him and everything. And now Mummy is not Happy Mummy and ARGH NO FAIR IT IS LIKE NOT EVEN MY FAULT THIS TIME.

UPDATED: He has phoned. He is still a git. Mum says, "He did explain" in a sort of useless hopeful way. Have had pie now, though.

COMMENTS

**frantastica**

Oh no! And she was so sweet and adorable about him yesterday!

**serafina67**

I know! Thank you for putting up with her Mummying you, btw. She is a bit madcakes at the mo, but in a sort of comedy dopey way. Apart from now obvs. Grr.

**frantastica**

Nonono, it was lovely. Mine is all prickly at the moment.

**serafina67**

*sends protective cushions*

**cameraobscurer**

Tosswit. I bet he rocks up tonight with a stupid bunch of flowers and thinks that'll make it ok.

**serafina67**

He will have to get through me first. *growls*

Also: ooh, you are back from ... wherever it was you went!

**cameraobscurer**

Ooh, yes I am! Gossip me up, am out of the loop.

**serafina67**

I got a white chocolate Easter egg shaped like a duck?

I lose at gossip. :(

**cameraobscurer**

Score!

**daisy13**

That's really sad. Were you looking forward to seeing him?

Or just worried about your mum?

**serafina67**

I was looking forward to him bringing me chocolate. *is shallow*
I have only met him that one time, so it is for Mum I am upset.
And also cos now I have panic that it is me that is the reason
he never comes over here, because I think Mum feels a bit
uncomfy about snogging his face off on the sofa when I am
watching telly. Due to me feeling a bit uncomfy with that too.
Erk. Feel bad now. Maybe should talk to Mother and
promise to be Nice at him. So long as she does not want
me to call him Unkie Ray and have my hair ruffled I can
manage that.

---

9.22 p.m. Monday 9 April | **forgivenesses!**

Ladies and gentlemen of ULife, I give you: Raymondo!
    *applauses*
    Observe as he drives up in his nice car with flowers ~~like how
Cam said he would~~! Gasp as he also gives her some chocolates
like you can buy at a garage! Mock as he attempts to give
serafina67 a kiss on the cheek, who runs away squeaking and
then remembers she is meant to be Nice and ends up having to
sort of chase him and give him a hug instead!
    It is more ITV sitcom than grand romance with Keira Knightley in
it, but at least Mum is smiley again.
    And they went out for food and I was invited, but I said nonono
must stay here with my tasty Lettuce Leaf Surprise etc so they

could go and be handholdy. I am so Nice it hurts. Apart from the part where I played VERY LOUD MUSIC all afternoon and then Della came down and shouted at me but only after I had been annoying her for like three hours. Oops.

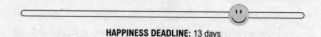

**HAPPINESS DEADLINE:** 13 days

COMMENTS

**cameraobscurer**

What do I win?

**serafina67**

Ummmm. Keira Knightley?

**cameraobscurer**

*politely turns her down* No offence but … no.

**serafina67**

lolz.

**frantastica**

Hurray! I was worried I might have to help you beat him up. I am not particularly good at that sort of thing.

**serafina67**

Thank you for the offer of your tiny little fists, though. :)

---

8.44 p.m. Wednesday 11 April | **Cindersera SHALL go to the ball!**

I have been putting it off and putting it off and hanging other things on the back of my door over the top of it, but Mum kind of pointed out this morning that the wedding is ON FRIDAY and my train goes TOMORROW NIGHT and I had probably better try on the Evil Drag Dress From Hades to check it still fits.

Which obvs sounded like WTF SERA YOU WILL BE GOING IN A BINBAG DUE TO YOUR HUGENESS to my small daft ears (not to mention OMG OMG FRIDAY WAAH etc). So there was much flailage and me sending her off to work before I got even as far as taking it off the hanger. And then a lot of trying to do up the zip with my eyes closed. (SHUSH.) And then some wriggling about and trying it with different knickers and, um, boob-floofing. BUT

*gasps*

It is not actually horrible?

I put it on again (with sparkly earrings gakked from frantastica and big piley-up hair) to show Mum when she came home, and it is not just my head playing tricks. She was all deranged and almost weepy. (Which, um, hello sera, you win NIL POINTS for sensitivity re weddings etc, but still, yay.)

I mean obvs it would look a million times nicerer on someone less hidjus. And I am still lumpy in places I am not supposed to be. (In fact I have checked scales and am, er, exactly ONE POUND lighter than I was when me and the Monster went shopping. Srsly. *headdesks*) And I totally will fall over in the magnificent shoes because I am carp at being, you know, a GIRL.

But, um, woo?

**HAPPINESS DEADLINE:** 11 days

COMMENTS

**frantastica**

*snugs you*

**serafina67**

*snugs both you and your earrings*

**cameraobscurer**

Yes lovely dear how super WHERE ARE THE PICTURES HMM?

**serafina67**

I EXPECT SOMEONE WILL TAKE SOME AT THE WEDDING. WHY ARE YOU SHOUTING AT ME?

**cameraobscurer**

I AM EXCITED ABOUT YOU BEING ALL PRETTY

**serafina67**

I AM EXCITED NOW TOO. WERE THERE DRUGS IN MY TEA OR SOMETHING?

**georgia darkly**

Sparkly inside = sparkly outside? :P

**serafina67**

Yay! (Though glittery intestines sounds yucky.)

**daisy13**

That's great!! It's really nice to hear you sounding so happy. I knew you'd look beautiful. Can't wait to see you in those pictures!!

**serafina67**

TY! It is so weird, I have been dreading this for like ever. And especially having people looking at me and wanting to take photos cos all the photos there are of me usually are of my hand over my face while I go "Argh stop taking my picture". But I am not going to do that this time. I am going to be all grown up and sensible and yay because I will actually look nice for the first time in the history of, um, history.

I really hope there weren't drugs in my tea. It would suck if it turns out I have been hallucinating.

---

12.07 p.m. Thursday 12 April | **\*wibbles\***

eeek argh waaaah omg

have to get train in like two hours

am too scared for capital letters

must not freak out on train

must not freak out at hotel

must not freak out tomorrow

must be Magic Perfect Beautiful Princess Sera

omg i am a bit scared now

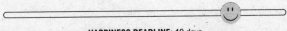

**HAPPINESS DEADLINE:** 10 days

COMMENTS

**frantastica**

Good luck sweetie!

**cameraobscurer**

Just be your awesome self. And if that stuffs up, JUST BE

YOUR AWESOME SELF. :-D
**rishyish**
Good luck!
**georgia darkly**
You will knock em dead, dude.
**daisy13**
*hugs*

---

10.48 p.m. Saturday 14 April | **THE WEDDING OMG**

Um. So. Wedding was yesterday and I was too ~~drunk~~ emotional to write anything down on Friday night, so I wrote most of this on the train on the way home and it was going to be only GOOD, honest. And then … um.

## The Good

INTRODUCTORY TINKLY MUSIC: *Twinkle twinkle sera star, you go on a train so far*

   A TRAIN STATION. A GOOD-AT-TRAINS GIRL SKIPS OFF THE PLATFORM INTO THE ARMS OF HER LOVING PAPA.

| | |
|---|---|
| PAPA: | Oh hai! UR luvly! |
| SERA: | Hello. I will overlook you talking like that as it is your wedding day and I am being well-behaved. |
| PAPA: | LOLZ! |

CUT TO: POSH BEDROOM IN POSH HOTEL, NEXT MORNING.

SERA IS BEING WELL BEHAVED AT HER SOON-TO-BE STEPMONSTER, WHO IS DRESSED IN A QUITE-NICE-ACTUALLY IVORY DRESS THING WHICH IS NOT AT ALL CAKE-RESEMBLING.

| | |
|---|---|
| MONSTER: | Oh hai! U can has halp me with hairs nao plz? |
| SERA: . | Clearly I will not be good at that but thank you for the bonding opportunity. Also: seriously, wtf is with the talking? |
| MONSTER: | We is nervous and trying to make U feel relaxed? |
| SERA: | You is are completely terrifying. Stop now? |
| MONSTER: | K! I can has something borrowed/blue from U pls? It R tradition? |
| SERA: | *thinks: today is going to be a long day* Here is my sock. |

CUT TO: SLIGHTLY LESS POSH BEDROOM IN POSH HOTEL. SERA IS IN HER HOLDING-IN KNICKERS AND HER CRAP BRA BECAUSE SHE FORGOT TO PACK THE SPECIAL NICE ONE OMG. (AUDIENCE IS REQUESTED TO WATCH THE FOLLOWING SCENE WITH EYES CLOSED.)

| | |
|---|---|
| SERA: | Hello reflection! |
| REFLECTION: | Hello! I look nicer with clothes on. Get dressed, you big silly. |
| SERA: | *puts on clothes* |
| SERA: | *puts on make-up* |
| SERA: | *puts make-up on clothes* |
| REFLECTION: | *eyerolls* |
| SERA: | Oh shush. You are not even supposed to talk. |

REFLECTION:   I was going to say you still look unexpectedly not-horrible, actually.

SERA:   Woo!

CUT TO: WEDDINGING! A LARGE ROOM WITH CHAIRS, FLOWERS, LOTS OF PEOPLE IN UNCOMFORTABLE SHOES/ HANDBAGS WITH COBWEBS ON. SERA SITS WITH DAD AS IF GIVING HIM AWAY. THIS IS WEIRD BUT NO ONE SEEMS TO NOTICE. A LADY PLAYS THE VIOLIN AS THE MONSTER COMES IN. ANOTHER LADY READS SOME STUFF OUT OF A BOOK. YAWNING OCCURS. ALSO PEOPLE CRY. DAD DOES A BIG SNOG ON THE MONSTER AND IT IS SORT OF EW BUT EVERYONE CLAPS SO SERAFINA DOES TOO. AND THEY BOTH LOOK QUITE HAPPY AND GLOWY AND ACTUALLY IT IS SORT OF HEARTWARMING IN A REAL AND ACTUAL WAY, NOT JUST LIKE ON THE TELLY.

CUT TO: MONTAGE! PHOTOS AND MORE PHOTOS AND SOME STANDING AROUND WHILE OTHER PEOPLE TAKE PHOTOS AND OMG YOU ARE LUCKY YOU ARE ONLY GETTING THE MONTAGE VERSION. ZZZZZ. SERAFINA IS BRAVE AND STRONG AND DOES NOT HIDE UNDER HER HAIR EVEN ONCE (MAINLY BECAUSE IT IS ALL TWIRLED UP ON THE TOP OF HER HEAD WITH FLOWERS IN).

CUT TO: DINNER! OR BREAKFAST AS THEY CALL IT BUT OMG YOU DO NOT EAT BREAKFAST AT 4 P.M. WHERE I COME FROM. MMMFOOD.

CUT TO: SPEEEEEECHES.

MR MONSTER: Gosh my daughter is beautiful she has always made me v proud like when she won lots of

|         |                                                                                                                      |
| ------- | -------------------------------------------------------------------------------------------------------------------- |
|         | gymkhanas when she was nine and when she got a scholarship and when she got into Cambridge and when she won some kind of a prize thing and now look she is beautiful and getting married at last yay *drinks champagne* |
| SERA:   | Wha? Who is this Monster lady and why do I not know any of these things?                                              |
| DAD:    | Gosh my new wife is beautiful and so is my daughter I love them both a very lot I am the luckiest man ever here are some jokes *drinks champagne* |
| SERA:   | Um. TY. *does not feel even at all sniffly, shush* Also when did you get to be good at speeches and making people laugh? |
| MR TIM: | Gosh I am the Best Man that means I need to have the Best Jokes uh-oh blah blah endless blah *drinks champagne* |
| SERA:   | Erk, did not need to hear THAT story omg. But champagne is yay!                                                       |

CUT TO: CRUMBLY DISCO. DAD AND MONSTER DO SLOW DANCE TO JAMES BLUNT. MR AND MRS MONSTER JOIN IN. MR TIM MAKES SERAFINA JOIN IN TOO. LUCKILY SHE HAS HAD CHAMPAGNE AND THUS DOES NOT CARE THAT HE IS MUNTY. DJ PLAYS "BANGING HITS OF 1987" FOR FOUR HOURS.

|          |                                                              |
| -------- | ------------------------------------------------------------ |
| MONSTER: | O hai RU having funz?                                         |
| SERA:    | Oh dear. I thought we had stopped talking like that.         |
| MONSTER: | It R a party! I has had boozes and gone MARRIED. LOLZ!       |

| | |
|---|---|
| SERA: | Yes you have. I am confusingly not cross with you. |
| DAD: | Oh hai RU having funz? |
| SERA: | Not you too. *sighs* Yes, Daddy. But only if you do not make me dance with Mr Tim again. |
| DAD: | ILU. |
| SERA: | ILU too. |
| DAD: | I kno I has had boozes but ILU rly for true. *hugs* |
| MONSTER: | I can has taking him away nao? |
| SERA: | Thank you. You are nice and rescuey. *hugs* |
| MR TIM: | I can has hugs too? UR pritty. |
| SERA: | I is going 2 bed, nightynight, no UR not invited, shoo. |

CUT TO: MORNING. SERA'S BEDROOM. CAVEMEN HIT SERA
ON HEAD WITH ROCKS TILL SHE WAKES UP.

| | |
|---|---|
| SERA: | Ow. |

CUT TO: HANGOVER BREAKFAST IN SAME ROOM WHICH
NOW LOOKS TOTALLY DIFFERENT AND IS CONFUSING.

| | |
|---|---|
| SERA: | Good morning Papa and ... Lady Who I Will Learn To Call Julia Without It Seeming Weird. |
| ~~MONSTER~~ JULIA: | Bacon and eggs yay! |
| SERA: | *voms* Um, what are you doing here, btw? Are you not supposed to be on honeymoon or something? |
| DAD: | We are going on Wednesday because it is cheaperer. |
| SERA: | How romantic. |

204

| DAD: | Have present? |
|---|---|
| SERA: | *unwraps little necklacey thing* |
| SERA: | *glees, guilts, glees* |

CUT TO: TRAIN STATION. SERAFINA STEPS ON TO TRAIN AND WAVES HER ~~HANDKERCHIEF~~ HAND AS SHE GOES OFF TO ~~WAR~~ HOME. AN INVISIBLE ORCHESTRA MAKES SWEEPING ROMANTIC NOISES. DAD AND JULIA SNOG AND THEN WAVE SOME MORE. SERAFINA IS ACTUALLY KIND OF OK WITH THAT.

## The Bad

*Up above the train so high, like an eejit in the sky*
ANOTHER TRAIN STATION. THE REALLY-VERY-GOOD-AT-TRAINS GIRL SKIPS ON TO THE PLATFORM.

| SERA: | Ho hum I am home again and have not died from weddinging. Yay! Now to find bus stop. |
|---|---|
| SERA: | *looks about platform* |
| SERA: | Oh look it is Ray. Hello Ray. |
| SERA: | *waves* |
| RAY: | *does not notice* |
| RAY: | *is busy* |
| RAY: | *is busy kissing a lady* |
| SERA: | *notices lady is not Mum* |
| SERA: | *quietly asplodes like pathetic little rabbit bomb* |

## The Ugly

*Twinkle twinkle crap sera, how I wonder WTF*

So I just went to the bus stop and didn't say anything, and he didn't see me so I don't think he knows I saw. And they were not like snogging. It was more of a sort of "obligatory wave lips and faces at each other and make hug-like movement" like what you do with rellies rather than people you actually like. But I do not think she looks very much like she might be his sister. Um. Now I have to tell Mum, y/n?

HALP?

I got in and was all "Um hi tired omg shower sleeeeep talk later kthxbai" and then just came straight here to post because ARGH I don't know what to do. Or I do know what to do but it is like life-ruining maybe. And I don't even know how to say it where I don't sound like Crazy Witch-Daughter who is making crap up and OMG I have just come back from Dad's WEDDING ffs how am I meant to do this now?

*cries for first time all weekend*

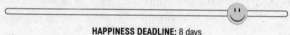

**HAPPINESS DEADLINE:** 8 days

COMMENTS

**daisy13**

I'm so sorry to hear that,

**frantastica**

I don't know what to say, honey. *hugs* is not at all good enough but have them anyway.

**cameraobscurer**

OMFG. Get him to tell her himself, the dog.

**temper temper**

Whoa nelly!

**georgia darkly**

Dude, that's just ... gah.

---

10.21 a.m. Sunday 15 April | **\*open mouth, hope sounds come out\***

I told her.

I could not sleep even though I only got like four hours of drunk!sleep the night before. But it just kept going round in my head with me thinking of nice ways to say something which is just not at all nice, so I just sort of wandered around and made cups of tea loudly till she woke up. And I said I needed to talk to her, and she wanted to go and have a shower, and I was just too tired to be sensible, so I just sort of said it without making it sound nice at all.

And she already knew.

He is married. She knows he is married. She knew he was married when they got together. I am a silly girl for worrying about it and it is none of my business.

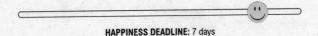

**HAPPINESS DEADLINE:** 7 days

---

Sorry for leaving comments off, needed to think for a bit. And then have a huge screaming row, apparently.

Mother says (in best UR-dumbass-child, me-talk-slooooooowly voice) that his marriage has been "virtually" over for years and he is planning to leave her "when the time is right" and he has only stayed for the kids (omg there are KIDS) and you don't choose who you fall in love with and I've studied Romeo and Juliet so I should understand and OMG WOMAN HOW STUPID ARE YOU? I am not even a grown-up and I know the I-will-leave-her-in-a-bit-only-not-yet is one of those things married blokes say and then never do. Apart from Dad obvs.

Um.

I don't know who I hate more, him for being a cheating git or her for being the one he is cheating with. Except I totally do because OMG she knows what it feels like when that happens to you because she has BEEN THERE. I don't even know her at all, do I?

Have not felt this awful in ages. And it is not even me that is in the wrong and it makes no difference. And she is in the kitchen crying and I am glad and I don't care how awful that makes me.

Comments still off because I am just telling you I am not dead or anything, I am just playing music VERY LOUDLY and hiding under the duvet. But TY for texts etc.

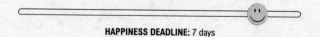

**HAPPINESS DEADLINE:** 7 days

Not going to school. Told her I was then waited for her to go and then came back. Sorry for not answering phone, Dad keeps trying to call and I can't talk to Mr Happy Wedded Bliss Man right now. Can't face people. Can't face anything.

She says she is going to discuss The Future with him at work today. Think she expects to come home going, "FU, unbeliever, he luffs me twuly and I have wrecked his marriage yay!" like that is meant to be a good thing. But I am ONLY A CHILD so wtf do I know.

Have found mostly full bottle of wine in fridge. That will be a nice lunch.

UPDATED: Mum is home. I am a selfish little girl who does not get to run her life or his. She is an adult woman who is quite capable of making her own decisions. THINGS around here are going to CHANGE.

I have no idea what this means. Except that she hates me.

UPDATED: Ray is telling his wife tonight. According to her, anyway. And from tomorrow they will live together in magic fairyland and ride round on unicorns, obvs.

Not sure where I fit in as I do not live in magic fairyland.

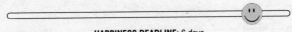

**HAPPINESS DEADLINE:** 6 days

COMMENTS

**frantastica**

Sweetie, I'm so sorry. Come to school tomorrow? You need people to talk to and.to not be stuck in your room. (And we

209

have French homework, but you probably don't really care about that right now.)

**rishyish**

That's messed up. Soz.

**cameraobscurer**

She needs a rocket up her, srsly. Don't go all Incidenty on us, babe, k?

**daisy13**

I wish I could do more than just *hugs*. I'm always here for you if you need someone, don't forget.

---

9.22 a.m. Tuesday 17 April | **5 days ha ha ha ha ha**

Still no phone call from Ray. She spent all night walking up and down and picking it up to check that it was actually plugged in. I spent all night wondering why him not calling is supposed to be my fault.

She has gone to work so I suppose she has her answer by now. OH GOSH UM I WONDER WHAT IT IS. *headdesks*

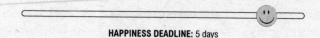

**HAPPINESS DEADLINE:** 5 days

---

| **oh god oh god oh god**

I don't know what to do. I really really totally don't know what to do.

Mum came home early from work. With Ray. And Ray's suitcase.

His wife has chucked him out which is MY FAULT and now he is going to be staying here which is MY FAULT and Mum isn't even happy about it because he is only here because he got thrown out not because he chose her and he probably doesn't even want to be here because no one would want to be here and they are hardly even speaking to each other ffs and OMG THIS ISN'T HAPPENING.

I can't believe this is my life. I am shaking so much as I'm typing this. I don't know what I'm supposed to do. I KNOW THIS IS YOUR HOME MOTHER SO YOU CAN DO WHAT YOU LIKE BUT I DO NOT HAVE ONE OF MY OWN BECAUSE I DO NOT HAVE A JOB BECAUSE I AM A CHILD. AND I AM YOUR DAUGHTER AND TO MOST PEOPLE THAT MEANS SOMETHING. AND I AM NOT THE ONE MOVING SOME TOTAL STRANGER IN AND OH EM GEE CAPSLOCK IS NOWHERE NEAR BIG ENOUGH.

I can't stay here. I can't live like this. I don't have anywhere else to go but I can't stay here. She is just slamming doors at me and talking about me really loudly so I can hear her saying the awfullest things. And I don't even know him and he will be in my home all the time with his scratchy red face and OMG.

I would put ~~>8:(~~ but it is not going to be ok in five minutes. Nothing is going to be ok, not in five minutes, not in five days either, not ever. I don't know what to do.

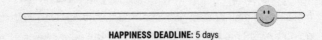

**HAPPINESS DEADLINE:** 5 days

## COMMENTS

**frantastica**

*hugs tightly*

I don't know what to say. That's awful. I really wish there was something useful I could do. Can you go and live with your dad? Or would that not be better?

**serafina67**

I don't know. I don't think so. He is going to Mauritius for three weeks from tomorrow. So that would be no, really.

**frantastica**

Maybe you could stay there while they're away?

**serafina67**

Like Mum is going to go for me being on my own for three weeks. And I wouldn't be able to get to school. And he would probably not let me anyway.

**cameraobscurer**

Who says they have to know? ;)

**serafina67**

If I do a bunk that's the first place Mum will look.

**cameraobscurer**

Duh. OK, fair point.

**frantastica**

What about when they get back? I know it means dealing with your mum and Ray for three weeks but at least you'd know it wasn't for ever.

**serafina67**

The Monster isn't going to want me hanging around and messing up their perfect guest bedroom. Actually Dad isn't going to want me hanging around either but he will say it's her so he doesn't have to feel bad. And everyone I know is here not up there anyway, and I would go totally totally beyond emo without friends. I'm screwed.

**georgia darkly**

Sorry, babe. That sucks.

**serafina67**

Yes it does.

**cameraobscurer**

WHAAAAAAAAAAAAAAT? BITCA.

You have to get out of there. You can't stay in a place where they pull that kind of crap on you.

**serafina67**

I know. But I don't have anywhere else to go.

**cameraobscurer**

If I could I would drag you over here in a heartbeat, you know that.

**serafina67**

I know you would. *loves*

**frantastica**

Oh god, me too. Only with Mike back there's no space and with how Dad is you would not be any better off. But I should've offered. That was really terrible of me.

**serafina67**

Nonono, not terrible, I know you would if you could and I know you have all your own stuff to deal with.

OMG, now this sounds like I'm grovelling for people's spare rooms to kip in and I'm not, I'm just saying I don't know what to do.

**cameraobscurer**

*hugs*

No one thinks that.

**8utterflywings**

I would flip out if that happened to me. That's like abuse or neglect or something. Can you put yourself in care or something?

**serafina67**

I don't know. I don't think so. I have two parents and I don't think the government cares that they are arseholes so long as they give me a place to live. And they are not beating me up or anything, they are just making me want to smash my head against the wall and gouge my eyes out.

**8utterflywings**

Maybe it's better if you stay. My cousin got taken into care and he ended up on smack.

**cameraobscurer**

If that's the most helpful thing you have to offer, maybe you should STFU.

**temper temper**

That's lousy. Parents suck. Do you have relatives you could stay with till things calm down? Because it sounds to me like the sort of thing that might seem less like the end of the world once you've had some time to think. I don't mean that in a kiss-off way, just talking from experience. Your mom probably feels really bad about all this, even if she isn't saying so.

**cameraobscurer**

So she should. I don't think her mum is really the one we should be worrying about right now.

**temper temper**

No, she isn't, but if we're trying to find a solution to the problem then we need to look at the whole picture and try to be sensible. No one can think straight when they're really upset. Talking about it like this just keeps making it worse and blows everything out of proportion.

### cameraobscurer

She's not blowing it out of proportion, dude. You have no idea what you're talking about.

### temper temper

None of us can know exactly how she feels. And that includes you, Cam. You don't speak to your dad and your relationship with your mom is totally FUBAR: doesn't make you an expert on family relations.

### cameraobscurer

WTF? Cheers for putting my private and personal details in someone else's comment thread. I never said this was about me. This is about sera and what's best for her. The people who are ACTUALLY HER FRIENDS are the ones who can help her figure that out. I don't see you riding in to save your Sudden Bezzie Mate.

### temper temper

If you were really interested in helping her find a way to live with this, you would be asking her how she feels, not bitching at me because you don't like it when I call you on your bullsh*t. You aren't here to help her. You just like the drama.

And I am not riding in to save her because I am in F***ING CHICAGO.

### frantastica

If you two want to get into a flamewar could you do it somewhere else? THIS IS NOT HELPING ANYONE.

### serafina67

I have an aunt in London, but she's my mum's sister so she would probably just send me back. And she has little kids and no space for a big fat one like me. And my grandparents are dead or nuts and live in like sheltered accommodation. So no.

**patchworkboy**

It's probably a bit weird for me to be here, so sorry, but I just wanted to say, I passed my test so if you want me to drive you somewhere I can do that. No strings.

**serafina67**

That's really kind of you, and I don't mind. I feel like I need all the help I can get right now. Only there isn't anywhere you can take me. That's the whole problem.

**patchworkboy**

If you change your mind, you know where to find me. *hugs*

**frantastica**

Are you still there? Do you want me to come over?

**serafina67**

No, it's ok. I would have to come out of my room and I don't really feel up for that. But thank you.

**lolbabe**

U def won't want me here either but soz etc? Hope UR ok?

**serafina67**

OMG. I don't even know what to say. Thank you. And same to you obvs.

**cameraobscurer**

Wanna run away to the circus?

I always wanted to be a trapeze artist. I think it's the spangly leotard. And you could be a lion tamer. With a parent-swatting whip. ;)

**serafina67**

You want to know the really pathetic thing? If running away to the circus was a thing you could actually do, I would do it right now.

**cameraobscurer**

Me too.

**serafina67**

I mean it, though. I would just go and not come back ever. I can't do this. I can't stay here. Mum keeps coming in and telling me I'm being a silly child and I need to stop crying and I keep trying and I can't.

I could skip the circus bit and just run away. I could just walk out of the door and go and not come back.

**cameraobscurer**

Go where?

**serafina67**

I don't care. Just not here.

Dad sent me money the other week for make-up and stuff for the wedding and I didn't spend it so I have some cash. Not enough for ages but enough for maybe a B&B for a few nights? And then I could get a job or something. And then I could disappear and no one would find me.

**cameraobscurer**

Won't you miss us?

**serafina67**

More than anything in the world.

**daisy13**

Are you serious?

**serafina67**

I am serious. I don't care if I never see Mum again. And Dad has his new life and probably won't even notice and it will be better for everyone if I just go.

**daisy13**

I honestly mean this:

Are you really, truly serious?

### serafina67

I will get on a train.

I will disappear and everything will be better.

### daisy13

Sarah, this is Dad.

Stay there. I'm on my way.

Love you. Xx

### cameraobscurer

*blinks*

OK?

What the shed is going on?

### frantastica

Honey, are you OK? I texted but I don't know if you have your phone.

*hugs* Only more than that, obviously.

### 8utterflywings

Is this for real? Because if it is for real, WTF?

Comment deleted by serafina67 7.09 p.m.

Comment deleted by serafina67 7.17 p.m.

Comment deleted by serafina67 7.24 p.m.

Comment deleted by serafina67 7.29 p.m.

Comment deleted by serafina67 7.40 p.m.

Comment deleted by serafina67 7.55 p.m.

Comment deleted by serafina67 7.59 p.m.

Comment deleted by serafina67 8.04 p.m.

Comment deleted by serafina67 8.05 p.m.

Comment deleted by serafina67 8.06 p.m.

Comment deleted by serafina67 8.09 p.m.

11.13 p.m. Tuesday 17 April | **Message from serafina67**

This is patchworkboy, posting here with sera's permission.

SERA IS OK. As in "not remotely OK", obviously, but she is at home, they are all talking to each other, they'll figure things out. Please stop calling the house, as you will only get me answering, and I have more important things to be doing, like ~~deleting comments~~ ~~fighting crime~~ making cups of tea.

She says thank you all for caring and not to worry. I say thank you all for blethering about this online, as I'm sure being Internet Faymus and having an inbox full of spam from strangers is absolutely what sera needs right now. </gigantic irony voice>

Now kindly bugger off. This is her place, not yours.

**HAPPINESS DEADLINE:** 5 days

COMMENTS

**cameraobscurer**

patchworkboy to the rescue! Or to the teapot, which is kind of the same thing. Wondered who it was that finally hit the "comments off" switch.
*snogs everyone*
And yeah, sorry, duh. Shutting up now, promise.

**frantastica**

Thank you for letting us know. *hugs to all* And I'm really sorry for calling and all of that. We were just worried and I didn't know what else to do. I'll delete what I put up at mine because that was probably stupid. Sorry. *feels awful*

**o jon o**

Cheers mate.

**8utterflywings**

I call TROLL.

**georgia darkly**

IDK. From what I've read, her dad is kind of an asshat. He could be an asshat online too.

**8utterflywings**

I meant the "I am not her I just happen to have her password" guy. But, whatever.

I call ASSHAT DAD.

**rishyish**

*hugs sera* I'm not going to pretend to have the faintest idea what's going on, but I hope you're all right.

**fishsquids5**

Wait, your dad is one of your ULife friends? That's messed up, dude.

**georgia darkly**

I think her dad is one of her friends and she didn't know. Messed up doesn't exactly cover it.

**fishsquids5**

Yowza. I thought my parental lunacy was pretty amped but that is like some kind of internet classic.

**adapted i**

Hi, I don't really know you, just wanted to say this all sounds scary and I hope you are OK!

**free milly**

So this is another internet fakeout thing by some corporation, yeah? *yawns*

**rishyish**

No, this is actually someone's life.

**georgia darkly**

We don't know that for sure. The dad thing could totally be

made up.

**frantastica**

We know sera in RL. It's not made up.

**georgia darkly**

So you say. You could be anyone.

**free milly**

Are you my daddy? :D

**georgia darkly**

NO LUKE I AM YOUR FATHER.

**gingerbread_ed**

I'M SPARTACUS!

**rishyish**

Am I the only one feeling super-paranoid now? I'm going to have to delete my entire life.

**fishsquids5**

omg totally! I would die if my dad read my blog.

**rishyish**

But how do you know he hasn't? *sets brain to panic mode*

**o jon o**

How about she deletes her dad instead? ;)

**rishyish**

That's going to happen anyway though, right? She's never going to forgive that.

**frantastica**

I don't mean to sound like I think what he did was ok, but he's still her dad. She can't just decide not to see him.

**cameraobscurer**

Why not? Dads do that disappearing crap all the time and their only excuse is being old and alcoholic and probably forgetting where I live. Him being creepy stalker dude = totally legitimate ditching.

**temper temper**

Is that the Poor Cam orchestra I can hear?

**cameraobscurer**

Dude, are you still here?

**o jon o**

No, she is in F***ING CHICAGO.

**cameraobscurer**

*snerts*

**rishyish**

Word. Blogstalking should be an arrestable offence. Except if they want mine to be used in evidence, in which case I was never here and I never said anything, your honour.

**frantastica**

Can we stop talking about this as if it is EastEnders?

**rishyish**

My bad, sorry. This sort of turned into the Online Trauma Help Desk in my head.

**cameraobscurer**

Dial 999, my blog is on fire!

**rishyish**

Is anyone else still here?

**georgia darkly**

So what happened?

**georgia darkly**

Is this thing dead now?

**georgia darkly**

HELLOOOOO?

**frantastica**

Are you coming back online anytime soon, honey? We miss you.

Once upon a time there was a girl, and a witch, and a princess, and they all lived together inside the same skin. Probably there were other people in there too, but the skin of one person is only so big, and already there were lumps and bumps sticking out in funny places from there being so many people inside. So Serafina Glassrhino (brown eyes, black hair, except for the bits where it was growing out) squashed the rest into her elbows and her toenails and behind her ears, where they couldn't cause trouble or be in the way, and mostly forgot they were even there at all.

One day a miserable bee came along, and stung the girl, and made her miserable. (That is what miserable bees do. This is why people hate them and run away squeaking.) So the princess and the witch had to go on a Quest to find her a Happiness which would cure her again. Neither of them was very sure what a Happiness looked like (the princess thought it would be a sort of golden bucket with emeralds, rubies etc stuck on it, which the witch thought was kind of pathetic, but then witches are not much good with happy things), but they were sure they would know it when they found it.

So the witch and the princess went off on all sorts of adventures which probably sound exciting and fun but were rubbish when you actually had to do them, while the girl stayed at home, doing homework and being cross, with her Mum-Queen, in their tall skinny castle-ish tower.

Almost a year went by, and the girl was still stung. The princess had found a Patchwork Prince to do rude things with, and then lost him again. The witch had learned there were times when she should just shush, although she still wasn't very good at it. And the girl lay in bed and talked to the sky and the ickle birdies and the daisies that grew by the moat about everything everything everything, because Complete Total Honesty was supposed to be a good bee repellent. But still there was no Happiness, shaped like a golden bucket or otherwise.

"OMG," said the girl, "I know they do not exactly fit into this sort of thing but I have like GCSEs soon and everything. Um, hurry up?"

And then one day her world asploded, which was quite unfair what with it already being quite complicated.

The tall skinny tower had a scratchy-faced Big Bad Wolfcutter living in it all of a sudden. The Dad-King (who had just married a dragon, which was a bit scary, even though she really wasn't very bitey or flamey) revealed he had been sitting on the doorstep of the tall skinny tower all along, listening to the Complete Total Honesty with all the rest, and pretending he hadn't. And now everyone everywhere seemed to be peering in through her windows and knocking on her door, to poke inside her head and ask her questions, which suddenly somehow seemed to be her own fault. Truly, there were not duvets big or thick enough in the whole castle for Serafina Glassrhino to disappear underneath.

Until …

"Tada!" said the Patchwork Prince, leaping over the moat below. "I have ridden here on the noble stallion MyMum'sVectra to save the day. Let down your hair, ~~Rapunzel~~ Serafina, and I shall climb up and make everything betterer."

"Um, OK," she said, because the witch still felt completely blargh about the whole thing on the beach, and the princess still hadn't told him how much she liked his New new hair, and the girl just sort of missed him. So the Patchwork Prince climbed up and made everyone tea, and things did get a little bit betterer.

"Tada!" said the Big Bad Wolfcutter, waving his phone about. "You people are all kind of alarmingly messed up and I am going to stay in a hotel for a bit, which will make everything betterer."

"Um, OK," said the Mum-Queen. (Probably. She was crying a lot and it was hard to tell.) So he went away, and the girl and the Mum-Queen had a proper talk, with only a little bit of crying, and once again things got betterer.

"Tada?" said the Dad-King, who was shaking and grey like never before, and also dragonless. "I have driven at illegal speeds to come and say sorry. Because I am sorry. I missed you and it seemed like a harmless thing and then I didn't know how to stop. And I love you. And I am sorry to the point of not even going to Mauritius which I hear is very nice at this time of year. Forgivenessing now?"

"Um, I will have to think about that," said the girl and the witch and the princess, all at once, because it was true. But even that made things feel a little bit betterer.

And so it went on. The Patchwork Prince rode over daily on MyMum'sVectra and made many more cups of tea. The Big Bad Wolfcutter went back to Mrs Wolfcutter in a totally predictable way, and the Mum-Queen seemed to think that was probably not such an awful thing after all. The Dad-King stayed for a week, until even the witch thought he should go to Mauritius before the dragon dumped him, so he did, but only after lots more apologizing. Lots of other lovely and unexpected people came to eat biscuits in the kitchen and give hugs, too. And everyone decided that Serafina Glassrhino would be quite all right.

But when April 22nd finally arrived, Serafina Glassrhino wondered why she could still feel the sting of the miserable bee when this was obvs the bit where they lived Happily Ever After. So she went to the laptop, and sat there just looking at it for a bit, wondering what to do and feeling a bit uncomfy. The princess told her how to be a good girl. The witch tempted her sideways. But the girl realized today she was just a girl, all alone, with no one but her left to decide what to do next.

So the girl chose. The girl left the princess and the witch, and even Serafina Glassrhino behind. She picked out a shiny new name for herself (which took ages because all the good ones are taken, srsly), and started again somewhere quiet and peaceful, where she could be ... oh, but that would be telling. :P

When she had finished peeling off that lumpy old skin, the girl who was not Serafina any more waited for the Golden Bucket of Happiness to appear, as if by magic, in the middle of the room.

It didn't. But the girl who was not Serafina sort of understood. And anyway the Mum-Queen bought her a kitten, which is totally win.

**HAPPINESS DEADLINE:** 365 days

## Trainful of Spidermonkeys, or
## How not to be Internet Famous for stupid/embarrassing/scary reasons

OK, so as we all know the internet is for CAPSLOCK. And lols. And general existingness. But also sometimes it is for scary people to lie to you, and maybe much much worse. So there are things you should Just. Not. Do online, like put your real name and address and phone number and pics of yourself in your bra in your public profile where just anyone can find them.

Obvs now you are all 'wtf we have heard this lecture and are not epically thick ~~like you~~ *eyerolls*' etc. Or maybe you think that being Internet Famous would be kind of win. (YOU ARE WRONG. It is unfun, trust me, and I did not even have anything all that awful happen to me really.) But even if you have nine million different social network accounts and usernames and avatars and are so l33t it hurts, sometimes you kind of forget that things that happen online are still *real*.

Um. So. It's sort of like this: in ye olden days of the internet they used to call it the Information Superhighway (lolz) like it was some magic road to The Amazing Shiny Future. But I think it's more like a train. You are in one carriage, with your friends, all talking about CDs/spidermonkeys/fit History teachers/leg hair/other very significant things. And it is totally a private conversation, even though there are loads of other people on the train who can hear you. (Actually, if you are honest, you quite like knowing the other people can hear you, because we all want to be listened to sometimes.)

Anyway this girl sitting across from you turns out to like spidermon-keys just as much as you do, and you get to talking, and it is awesome good to have this new spidermonkeyish friend. And there's a cute guy sitting in the next seat: yay! More friends. Then the lady sitting behind you reminds you about the leg hair conversation, which suddenly seems like a bad idea now there's this cute guy here. And then down the carriage someone gets up to go to the loo and you realise it's the fit History teacher, who looks at you all peculiar what with you all having been talking about his bum for like an hour. Zomg embarrassing, especially now all your friends are saying it was you that started it. Then you spot this creepy guy in the corner, who's just staring, like he's memorising every word you say.

So you get off the train, and you realise as you stand on the platform looking at the people in the carriage that they all know your name and your face and what you look like in your bra, and maybe even where you live – because you told them. And the leg hair and History teacher and mean friends stuff might be zomg embarrassing, but if the creepy guy wants to get off the train and follow you home, behold how much carp you could be in.

Trains are good. They can take you to interesting places. Just don't forget that you're on one, k?

**Sarah Jayne Duffy** xx
(see what I did there? Don't do that. :P)

**Good places to find out stuff**

http://www.thinkuknow.co.uk/ has loads of really brainy advice, like not putting pics of yourself in school uniform up so pervy types can't figure out where you live. There's a button you can click if you want to report anything that happens online that you think is dodgy.  And there are bits for grown-ups too, so they can grow a clue about online-type stuffs.

http://www.bbc.co.uk/chatguide/ has info for blokes as well as girls, and loads about how to deal with online bullying.

http://www.fkbko.co.uk is For Kids By Kids Online, so there's lots about texting, gaming, chat etc as well as social networks and blogs.

http://www.connectsafely.org/ has a forum for adults to ask for advice, and is supported by all the big social networks.

http://www.childline.org.uk/ is a free helpline for children and young people in need: you can call them on 0800 1111 about cyberbullying or if you think someone online might be trying to harm you.

## tyvm :D

So many people have helped serafina and co climb out of my laptop. Huge thanks to Caroline Walsh and Maggie Evans, for repeatedly putting a daft grin on my face last year. Biggest Woo to Marion Lloyd, Rachel Griffiths, Sarah Lilly, Andrew Biscomb and all the Scholastic superheroes, for such spectacular enthusiasm and arsekickery. Supermassive hugs to my family, especially my sisters Tina, Nicky and Jess, for being honest as well as kind. And much love (and curry) to the 'Talents': Ruth Eastham, Zoe Finney, Josie Henley-Einion, Caroline Johnson, and Sarah Mussi.

Most importantly, thank you to all the anonymous Beboers, Bloggers, Facebookers, Habbo Hoteliers, MySpacers, Livejournalists, and all the rest. Yes, you can has cheezburger.